D0290046

FLIGHT FROM FELICIDAD

Guilty of murder, Old Man Hennessey is in the Felicidad jail awaiting the hangman. However, Frank and Jack O'Connor break him out, needing his help in carrying out a robbery. Then, in an act of revenge on the town, Hennessey kidnaps Thora Dowling, the marshal's fiancée, and Lizzie, a prostitute. On his trail are Marshal Kirkpatrick and Elias Pitt, hoping to prevent Hennessey's escape to Mexico. But more importantly, will they be in time to rescue Thora and Lizzie?

STEVEN GRAY

FLIGHT FROM FELICIDAD

Complete and Unabridged

LINFORD
Leicester

First published in Great Britain in 2007 by
Robert Hale Limited
London

First Linford Edition
published 2008
by arrangement with
Robert Hale Limited
London

British Library CIP Data

Gray, Steven
    Flight from Felicidad.—
    Large print ed.—
    Linford western library
    1. Western stories
    2. Large type books
    I. Title
    823.9'14 [F]

    ISBN 978–1–84782–319–9

Published by
F. A. Thorpe (Publishing)
Anstey, Leicestershire

Set by Words & Graphics Ltd.
Anstey, Leicestershire
Printed and bound in Great Britain by
T. J. International Ltd., Padstow, Cornwall

This book is printed on acid-free paper

1

The two riders approached the ranch cautiously. Just in case. But the ramshackle house and the dusty yard were quiet in the heat of late morning. Nothing moved; there were no sounds.

'Hell and damnation!' Frank O'Connor pulled his horse to a halt. He took off his hat and wiped away the sweat from his neck then stared across at his brother. 'Hell, I really don't believe this. I was sure we'd find the family here, alive and kicking, and planning their next rustling raid across the border.'

Jack shrugged. 'It certainly don't look like anyone is home. There ain't no horses in the corral. No one's done come out to greet us.'

'Hell, greet ain't exactly the word I'd use. Any one of the Hennesseys was in the house they'd've been out by now, guns at the ready.'

The brothers grinned at one another. At 45 Frank was the older by five years. While they weren't much alike — Frank was tall and thin with long black hair that had a bald spot in the middle, whereas Jack was plump with very short hair — both had bad teeth and stubbly beards and both were always in need of a bath. They were part-time outlaws who weren't quite as successful as they considered themselves.

'Best make sure.' Jack dismounted and walked, a little nervously, up to the door of the house, hand hovering over the butt of his gun.

The door opened to his touch revealing dust and filth. He saw an upturned chair, chipped and dirty crockery lying on a table, a whiskey bottle, empty more was the pity, and creatures that skuttled and slithered away in the sudden beam of hot light. He turned back and shrugged again.

'Well?' Frank demanded.

'Looks like the stories we done heard in Nogales were true.'

Stories they'd hotfooted it here to disprove.

Frank took a quick drink from his canteen. The water tasted warm and brackish. 'They can't be.' He sounded incredulous.

'Ain't no one here. The place is deserted and looks like it has been for a while.'

Frank shook his head, feeling bewildered. It didn't seem possible. If everything was true it meant the Hennessey clan was no more. That Bobby-Jo and Belle were dead, together with Belle's husband, Charley Burchell, and Larry Leapman, their foreman. And, the biggest shock of all, that Old Man Hennessey, the leader of the clan, had been caught, tried and sentenced, and was now in jail awaiting the hangman.

It meant that the Hennesseys had, at last, been bested by the law. And not just any law but by the Marshal of Felicidad who was a damn Eastern greenhorn.[1]

---

[1] See Fight at Felicidad

'No,' he muttered.

'Hell, Frank, whether the clan was rustling over in Mexico or running the stolen cattle into Texas they never left the ranch deserted. Someone'd be here.' Jack grinned. 'Belle, most probably, moaning like she always did 'bout how the men got to do all the exciting things and she got to do the cooking and cleaning.'

Not that Belle's cooking or cleaning had ever been up to much.

'Yeah. Oh, hell!'

'What we goin' to do?' A whine entered Jack's voice as he walked across to his brother. 'We was depending on getting the Hennesseys to help us. It's too risky to pull off the robbery by our lonesomes. We ain't giving it up, are we?'

'Course we ain't. Not if we can help it. We stand to gain too much money for that. More money, Jack, than we've ever seen afore.'

Frank and Jack had been riding to the Hennessey place to ask if Bobby-Jo and Leapman would care to take part in the robbery they'd been planning for several months. That was how they'd ended up in Nogales where rumours were flying about concerning the demise of the clan.

'Anyway we oughta help Bernie if we can,' Frank added. 'He is some sorta cousin of ours after all.'

Jack's eyes lit up greedily. 'So?'

'So, first off we ride on into Felicidad, find out if all this is true and if Bernie is in jail, waiting to swing on the gallows.'

Jack nodded nervously and ran a hand over his windpipe. He didn't like talk about hanging. He was well aware that if he and Frank were caught they'd done enough bad things to receive the same sentence.

'And if he is?'

'Well then, Jack, we break him out! Didn't Bernie always say there weren't no jail big enough to hold him?' Frank laughed. 'Seems like we're 'bout to help him prove it.'

'Are you certain that's what we oughta do? Bernie ain't goin' to be pleased 'bout what's happened.'

And when Old Man Hennessey was displeased it was best not to be anywhere near him.

Frank had his own doubts but he pushed them aside. 'Remember, we rescue him he's goin' to be real grateful. So grateful he won't refuse to help us.'

Jack grinned. As he mounted his horse he patted one of his saddle-bags and said, 'Good thing we worked in the mining industry for a while.'

'Yeah,' Frank agreed. 'You just never know when these things'll come in handy. C'mon, let's go. I hope we ain't too late.'

2

'You won't never hang me.' Old Man Hennessey clutched the bars of his cell, his knuckles standing out white and knobbly. He sneered at Marshal Kirkpatrick, stretching the scar on his left cheek out of shape as he did so. 'You might've killed my kids, but you ain't about to kill me. 'Less it's with this godawful muck you call dinner.'

He kicked at the plate and cup sending them flying out of the cell and across the narrow corridor where they hit the wall with a clatter.

Kirkpatrick bent to pick up the crockery and made Hennessey laugh when he winced as he did so. The bullet wound incurred in the bloody shoot-out with the clan, and for which he still wore his arm in a sling, was healing and it no longer hurt, except for a painful twinge now and then when he moved awkwardly like he had then.

Leaning against the cell door, he said, 'I'm sorry about Bobby-Jo and Belle but they deserved what happened to them. And, Bernie, so do you.'

'Sonofabitch! You'll be sorry for this, you see if you ain't. And so will that damn girlfriend of yours too.'

'I've heard all your threats before. They don't worry me. But if you say any more about Miss Dowling then by God I'll give you something to worry about.' Kirkpatrick pointed a finger at Hennessey and then turned away. At the doorway to his office he glanced back.

Left by himself the fight had gone out of his prisoner. Hennessey had slumped back on the bunk, leaning against the lumpy pillow. He looked scared. Scared not just of hanging, but of having to face the town he and his family had once terrorized, with a noose around his neck.

Kirkpatrick wasn't going to waste any undeserved sympathy on the man. In fact he was pleased that Hennessey was now frightened of the townspeople and frightened of dying. The Old Man had got away with his violence and law-breaking for far too long and deserved his fate.

Kirkpatrick wasn't quite so pleased that the hanging was still two days away.

The jury's verdict and Judge Corbett's sentence had both been foregone conclusions. As soon as the judge announced Hennessey was to hang, Kirkpatrick wanted the execution to go ahead. But Corbett said the proper procedures must be followed, the proper gallows built and a proper hangman brought in.

He decreed that the hanging should take place in five days' time — five long days during which something could go wrong.

But, as he went to the window and looked out on the crowded but peaceful street, Kirkpatrick thought he was worrying unnecessarily. So far everything was going right.

The gallows being erected by the side of the court-house were almost built. That morning he'd received a message to say the hangman was on his way from Santa Fe. And he had no fears that the townsmen would take the law into their own hands and try to lynch the Old Man. They'd lived in the shadow of the Hennessey brood for so long that now they wanted the law to take its rightful course and for Hennessey to be hanged legally while they all looked on.

Besides, a great number of people had travelled into Felicidad from the ranches, farms and hamlets roundabout for the excitement of the trial and almost all of them were staying on for the even greater excitement of the hanging. More men, women and children were arriving each day and other thrill-seekers were travelling miles to get here. For Hennessey's name was well known, not only in this part of New Mexico, but Arizona and Texas as well. Mexico too, of course, for that country had been plagued by the clan's regular rustling expeditions.

Felicidad was making a good deal of money from the out-of-towners and the citizens were happy and eager to make more. They wouldn't give all that up for the momentary pleasure of lynching Hennessey.

Those ranchers and their men still out on cattle drives and who wouldn't make it back in time would be angry at what they'd missed. They would have to be content with reading the reports in the town newspaper and buying copies of the pictures taken of the corpses by the paper's photographer. He'd already sold dozens of those of Bobby-Jo and Belle and had asked that he be allowed to take one of Hennessey hanging from the gallows. Kirkpatrick couldn't see any reason to deny him his request.

The office door opened and Kirkpatrick looked up as his plump deputy, Dave Vaughan, came in.

'All quiet?'

'Yeah,' Vaughan said with a little nod.

'At the moment. But the saloons are clearly getting ready for another night of wild abandon.' He took off his hat and eased himself into his chair. 'We'll be busy again.'

'Yeah I guess.'

'Hennessey?'

'Moaning as usual.'

The two men looked at one another and grinned.

'Dave, you mind if I take the opportunity to pay Miss Dowling a visit?'

'No, go ahead,' Vaughan agreed, smiling.

'I won't be long.'

Thora Dowling was Kirkpatrick's fiancée and it was thanks to her that Old Man Hennessey was going to pay the final penalty.

On her way from Pennsylvania to join Kirkpatrick in Felicidad, she had witnessed Hennessey murder three men. Although understandably frightened, she had been determined to stand up in court and say what she had seen. The rest of the clan were equally determined that Hennessey should go free and had done their best to make sure she wasn't alive to testify. But with the help of Elias Pitt, a gambler who had sided with Kirkpatrick and so managed to get himself on the Hennessey hit-list, she had escaped their clutches.

Their plans thwarted, the clan then resorted to trying to break Hennessey out of jail. The result was a gun battle, after which the Old Man was the only Hennessey left alive.

Kirkpatrick had left home two years before to travel West and become a law officer. Hearing that the post of town marshal was vacant he'd ridden to Felicidad, and found a small but reasonably prosperous town in the foothills of the Mimbres Mountains, close to the border with Mexico. All round were hills covered with pine-trees that filled the air with their scent. There were stores grouped around a plaza, a tiny business district, and a good feeling about the place. He'd decided to apply for the position and being the only applicant, which should have aroused his suspicions, had been appointed.

At first, several of the citizens had expressed doubts that an Easterner would be up to the job, but he'd soon impressed them with his ability to work hard and keep the peace. Even when he found out about the Hennesseys and that they were the reason no one else had applied for the job, he hadn't minded: he liked both the town and the job. Things were even better now because since defeating the clan he was considered a hero. People were eager to pat him on the back, buy him a drink, seek out the details of the shoot-out.

Although he'd been upset at the killings he knew they had been inevitable and he'd decided he wanted to stay in the job. The townspeople were pleased with his decision. It helped that they liked Thora as well because what he wanted most of all was to marry her and move into their own home; begin their new life together.

Once the hanging was over he would at last be free to do so.

★　★　★

Left alone, Hennessey ran a hand through his stringy grey hair and stood up, pacing back and forth in his cell. How he hated being confined. How he hated the feeling of helplessness, of being locked up, and the fear that he had no choice but to sit here waiting to die.

Along with the threat of hanging — of dying — was the knowledge that those people he blamed for the downfall of himself and his family were going to get away with what they'd done. In the past he'd always punished those who'd dared do him down and he couldn't believe he wasn't going to get the chance to take his revenge on Felicidad.

Although most people believed otherwise, Old Man Hennessey hadn't killed that many men; he'd found his reputation alone was enough to terrorize his enemies. But since shooting Adam Mills and the other two men at the stage station he'd decided he liked killing and he wanted to kill Marshal Kirkpatrick, the gambler Pitt, and Thora Dowling, the very thought of whom made him break out into an angry sweat.

But he was having to come to terms with the possibility that he wouldn't be able to avenge himself on the town. For with each passing moment it seemed that his execution was more and more likely to take place and that he wouldn't be saved from the noose or the jeering mob who would come to watch him swing on the gallows.

3

The O'Connor brothers reached Felicidad in the middle of the afternoon. They'd immediately headed for the redlight district and now sat brooding over bad whiskey in Carney's Saloon. Of course it was no longer Carney's, because Jake Carney was dead, nor did it have the same sense of danger it once had, but it was still the sort of place in which they felt at home. Even better, it was almost empty so they could discuss their plans without being overheard.

All the streets of the town were crowded with various carriages and buckboards, horses were tied to hitching posts, and the sidewalks were full of pedestrians, shopping and gossiping.

So, as soon as they arrived, they knew that, farfetched though they seemed, the stories were true. Old Man Hennessey was in jail, awaiting the hangman, and townsmen, ranchers, farmers and the curious were eager to witness him breathe his last.

They'd managed to get hold of a copy of the local newspaper, *The Felicidad Times*, and Frank, who could just about read and write, had read out loud the lead article to Jack, who couldn't. It was accompanied by several photographs, including, they were both angry to see, several taken of the corpses of Bobby-Jo, Burchell, Leapman and even Belle, just after they'd been shot dead.

Frank tapped a photo depicting two men and a young woman.

'It seems these three are the ones what done it: Marshal Kirkpatrick, Elias Pitt, and Thora Dowling, the marshal's betrothed.' He stumbled over the unfamiliar words and Jack asked him what betrothed meant, which he didn't know but guessed it meant the pair of them were somehow friendly. 'They're being called heroes.'

'For killing Hennesseys,' Jack said

with a scowl. 'Don't seem right to me.'

'Nor me. Let's see. Yeah. The trial was held last Friday and the hanging's due on Wednesday morning.' Frank counted up on his fingers. 'That's the day after tomorrow, ain't it? We ain't got long. Fact, we'd better get him out today. We don't wanna take the chance of him being lynched.'

'OK.' Jack nodded agreement and gulped nervously. Lynch talk was the stuff of nightmares.

Besides, neither was happy to wait around in Felicidad too long, where the marshal, a local hero, might recognize them from a Wanted poster.

'What's the plan?'

Frank's face frowned in thought. 'We'd better steal three good horses from the livery. We rode our two hard to get here and they're just about played out.'

'Right.'

Most of the animals they rode were stolen.

'We'll find somewhere to leave 'em round the back of the jail where they won't be spotted and where they'll be waiting when we want 'em.'

'Frank, what building shall we use? What about The Silver Dollar?' Jack had heard stories of how Ned Wilkes, the owner, had once refused to serve Bobby-Jo. Not that he was ever likely to try to go in there because even from the outside it looked posh and forbidding.

'No, it's too far from the jail.'

'What about a bank?'

Jack thought it would be nice to rob a bank at the same time as breaking Hennessey out.

'It don't look like Felicidad has got one.'

'Pity.'

'But I did spot a large dry goods store owned by someone called Toombs. It's on a corner, quite near the jail, and it'll cause a real big sensation!' Both brothers laughed and Frank added, 'Give us plenty of time to rescue Bernie and get away safely.'

'Want another?' Jack indicated their empty glasses.

Frank nodded and waited until Jack bought two more whiskeys. 'Been thinking. The best time to do it would be at night, but it ain't a real good idea to be galloping out of Felicidad, down an unknown trail, when it's too dark to see what's in front of us. We do that we risk hurting the horses or ourselves, and letting a posse catch up.'

'But we can't rescue Bernie while it's light,' Jack objected. 'Someone'll see us for sure. We'll end up in jail too.'

Frank drained his glass and shook his head. 'Not if we do it when it's just on dusk. The stores will be shut up for the night and I bet the plaza'll be empty by then too. The saloons'll be getting into their swing and most folk will be there or at home. No one'll be around to take any notice of what we're up to. And it should still be light enough for us to ride away.'

'If you're sure.' Jack still sounded doubtful.

'Look at it this way: if someone is

around we can deal with him, can't we?'

Jack grinned.

'And iffen anyone's at the livery to try and stop us stealing horses they can be dealt with too! I guess we oughta find a way to let Bernie know we're here so he can be ready. Then we wait.'

'We got time to have a woman?' Jack glanced at the one whore still employed at the saloon. She was sitting with a couple of low-lifes at a nearby table. She looked bored and had winked at him a couple of times.

'Best not. We don't want nothing to go wrong and we've got a lot to do.'

Jack scowled. But he supposed Frank was right. Helping Old Man Hennessey escape and getting away from Felicidad was more important than enjoying the company of a woman, especially as he could have any number of women after the robbery. And if they didn't do it soon and do it right they wouldn't be able to do it at all.

4

Lizzie put down the piece of sewing on which she was attempting to work. She stared out of the parlour window of the boarding-house and sighed heavily.

'What's the matter?' Thora Dowling asked, looking up from her own embroidery.

'Oh, Miss Dowling, you're so lucky to have someone like Marshal Kirkpatrick love you. And you'll make him such a good wife.'

Although she earned her living as a prostitute and had few illusions about men, Lizzie was a romantic girl at heart. She never tired of hearing how Thora and Ralph had been childhood sweethearts and how, despite her parents' objections, Thora had followed him out to New Mexico all the way from Pennsylvania, wherever that was, braving difficult travelling conditions and outlaws to do so.

And Lizzie, who was a little in love with Ralph herself, thought he was so handsome with his brown hair and brown eyes and Thora, while not exactly pretty, was nice-looking, being a plumpish young woman of twenty-five who combed her brown hair into a tidy bun and wore good clothes. She always looked neat and tidy and she was respectable, which Lizzie didn't believe she could ever be.

'You're both so brave. He's a hero and you're a heroine. Everyone says so.'

'I just did my duty,' Thora objected, but all the same she smiled at the girl's words. And, yes, she admitted, she was lucky.

Her only worry over the future was that Ralph wanted to continue as Felicidad's town marshal, where he might have to risk his life to uphold the law. But then she told herself there would never be another man like Old Man Hennessey for him to go up against. There couldn't be. The thought

24

of the Old Man and all he'd done still made her shiver. And while she knew she must put everything that had happened out of her mind, she also knew she would never ever forget the elation, the pleasure, on Hennessey's face as he pulled the trigger of his gun and shot three men. Nor would she forget the terrifying ride through the hills when she and Elias Pitt were chased by the rest of the clan.

Even at his trial her ordeal wasn't over. Hennessey had kept his eyes fixed on her all the while she was giving her evidence against him as if he was committing to memory every single detail of her face.

Since her arrival in the town there had even been times when, although she loved Ralph, she wondered if her parents were right and she'd made a mistake in coming out here to marry him. Everything was strange enough — the heat and dust, the buildings made of adobe, the colourful characters she'd met — without the violence and lawlessness she'd found. But now surely everything was going to be all right and she could put her doubts behind her.

Remembering how Pitt had come to her rescue, she said, 'I'm sure you'll find someone of your own one day soon. What about Mr Pitt? He likes you, doesn't he? He calls in to see how you are nearly every day.'

'Elias is nice,' Lizzie agreed. 'I like him too. But once he's bored with Felicidad he'll move on. And he won't even consider taking me with him.'

Thora nodded sadly. 'You're probably right.'

Elias Pitt was a professional gambler, who drifted from town to town, looking for the best poker games. He had no ties or roots here; had made it clear he didn't like the thought of living in the same place forever or being responsible for someone else. He would soon want to try his hand at gambling elsewhere. And, she admitted, it was unlikely he would take Lizzie with him when he left. She wasn't the type of girl men married. She was the type they enjoyed and then forgot.

In Lizzie's case it was even worse because she came encumbered with the knowledge that Old Man Hennessey had once considered her his private property. It was her flirting with Adam Mills in Carney's saloon that had set off the chain of events leading to Hennessey's being sentenced to hang.

'I'm no homemaker. Look at this!' Lizzie held up the piece of sewing. 'I can't even stitch a straight seam. I can't cook. I barely know how to clean. And soon, when I'm better, Mrs Barron will turn me out and I'll have to go back to the saloons.'

'Oh, Lizzie.'

'Don't look at me like that, Miss Dowling, you know it's true. Mrs Barron doesn't approve of me or my staying here. She wants me to go as soon as possible.' Lizzie sighed a little. 'Not that I blame her for that.'

Lizzie was only here because Mrs Barron had once been a nurse during the Civil War and was the nearest thing Felicidad had to a doctor. And while Mrs Barron might not approve of prostitutes, her kind heart had not allowed her to turn Lizzie away after the girl was badly beaten by Jake Carney. But she'd made it plain that once Lizzie had recovered she must leave.

'At least you're free of Carney and Hennessey.' Both men had treated her badly.

Lizzie said, 'I won't feel really safe till Bernie is hanged.'

'It won't be long now and perhaps once it's over and you're better you can go to another town where no one knows you and there start anew.'

'Yeah,' Lizzie said with a little smile, but it was a sad smile as if she felt that was unlikely to happen.

At that moment Mrs Barron put her head round the parlour door. 'Thora, dear, Marshal Kirkpatrick is here to see you. He hasn't got very long.'

Thora's face lit up, making Lizzie

sigh again. She stood up, placing her sewing on the chair, and hurried out to the hall where Ralph waited for her.

★　★　★

'Bernie, Bernie, you there?'

The voice came from outside his jail cell. Hennessey got up and went over to the window. It was narrow and too high for him to see out of even if he stood on tiptoe.

'Who is it?' he called.

'It's us, the O'Connors. Frank and Jack. We're here to get you out. This evening.'

'You'd better,' Hennessey said, knowing the O'Connors were idiots who rarely succeeded in doing what they planned.

'We will. Be ready.'

Hennessey's ugly face broke into a grin. Because if they did rescue him then everyone would discover what exactly it meant to cross him.

5

Although the sky towards the west was still streaked orange and red with sunlight, the plaza was empty and the stores closed. Lamplight shone from the marshal's office and from the lobby of the hotel but otherwise the buildings were dark. It was quiet too, the only sounds coming from the direction of the red-light district.

Jack stood guard, looking out for anyone who might disturb them and being ready to shoot them too. And Frank set about placing the sticks of stolen dynamite against the wall of Mr Toombs's dry goods store.

'Get ready to run,' he called, as he lit the fuse.

★   ★   ★

Elias Pitt knew that the rancher sitting opposite him, the only other person left in this latest game of poker, believed he had a winning hand. But Pitt was pretty sure his cards would beat it, especially with the way they were falling for him. It seemed he couldn't lose. They had been playing since the middle of the afternoon and the other four men at the table had lost every game to him. So he raised the stakes again and waited for the man to meet the bet. He wasn't disappointed.

'Two pair, kings and tens,' the rancher said, sounding sure of himself.

Normally it would have been a good hand.

'Sorry.' Pitt laid down his own cards. 'I've got four nines.'

'Damn! Thought I had you beat there.' The rancher grimaced, sounding resigned and rueful. He gathered up the cards and offered them to the gambler to shuffle. 'Another?'

Pitt shook his head. 'Think I'll give it a rest for a while.' He scooped up his winnings, got to his feet and stretched.

'Good. At least that'll give one of us the chance to win for a change,' someone else grumbled. 'But I expect you'll be back.'

Pitt smiled and walked through the crowd to the bar where Ned Wilkes had a cold beer waiting for him.

'There you go,' Wilkes said.

Pitt took it gratefully, drank half in one swallow, and leaned back against the bar, staring round.

Even though it was still early evening the red-light district was already buzzing. In fact the saloons and brothels were busy more or less every hour of the day and night. Trade had never been so good and everyone — saloon-keepers and gamblers, brothel madams, the lone prostitutes — wanted to take advantage of the fact. And doing best of all, because it was where those with the most money went — the ranch owners rather than the cowboys, the more influential townsmen — was The Silver Dollar.

It stood on a corner, an imposing building with its name picked out in gold-leaf on the windows. Its floor was wooden, there was a bar made of mahogany with polished glasses displayed behind it, and the walls were decorated with paintings depicting battles between the US cavalry and Indians. And if Wilkes, the owner, didn't allow girls to ply their trade there, he did provide plenty of gambling: an ever busy roulette wheel and poker dealt by Elias Pitt. It was a good place for someone like him to be employed.

Pitt was thirty-three and looked exactly like the professional gambler he was. Tall and lean, he had blue eyes, black hair and a handlebar moustache. His favoured clothes were a black frockcoat, low heeled boots and dark trousers with a matching vest over a white shirt.

Seventeen years before he had quit the family farm on the mid-West Plains and headed further West to try his luck at cards. Where his skill at playing poker and other games of chance came from he didn't know, but he'd never had cause to regret his decision. He liked the life and he made a good living, too. The only shame was that he no longer had anything in common with his parents and two brothers, and his visits home were far between and fleeting.

He didn't need to cheat in order to win and, knowing he played a fair game, there was never any shortage of men lining up to do their best to beat him. While Wilkes took a share of the winnings, so much business had come his way these past few days, he was earning more than he ever had before.

All the same he intended leaving Felicidad once Old Man Hennessey was hanged.

He'd come to gamble in the town until the heat of the New Mexican summer so near the Mexican border drove him to the higher, cooler country around Santa Fe. Instead of the easy life he anticipated he'd found danger when he became involved with helping Marshal Kirkpatrick and Thora Dowling in their fight against the Hennesseys. While he never sought out trouble he didn't back away from it either and he'd little choice but to become further involved when the Hennesseys' anger was also turned on him.

It had spoiled Felicidad for him. He wanted to leave it all behind. And he had nothing to hold him here. Not even Lizzie. For he knew that as much as he liked her he wouldn't stay because of her.

Once the thrill of the hanging was over nearly everyone would be returning to their ranches and farms, the town would again be quiet and he could ride away without any regrets.

'Looks like it's gonna be another good night,' Wilkes said, pausing in helping his two barmen serve drinks. 'How you doing?'

'I had the beating of the table.' Pitt stared out at the heaving crowd.

'In one way it's a pity Hennessey is

hanging in two days time and all these people will be gone,' Wilkes said, thinking of the money he was making. He wiped down the bar. 'But it can't come soon enough for most folks.'

'Guess not.'

'We had to put up with that bunch of thugs for years. Most of us won't be happy till we know the last of 'em is dead and buried. I just hope nothing goes wrong.'

'Don't see that it can.'

Wilkes shook his head. 'Don't take nothing for granted where Hennessey is concerned.' Someone called for more beer and he turned away to serve him.

Thinking Wilkes was worrying over nothing, although he wasn't alone, most of the other towns-people shared the same concerns, Pitt finished his own beer. He was about to return to the poker table when the swing doors were pushed back and Marshal Kirkpatrick came in. Ralph was a young man in his twenties and of medium height but the way he wore his badge meant he had no difficulty in pushing his way through the crowd.

When Pitt first heard about Kirkpatrick he was worried that he was perhaps only playing at upholding the law and that as an Easterner, he wouldn't be up to handling a situation in which gunplay was likely. But Ralph had quickly proved his worth.

'Hi,' Pitt said, as the marshal reached the bar.

'Evening. Ned, let's have a beer. It's hot out there on the street and even hotter in here.'

'On the house, Marshal.'

'Thanks.' Kirkpatrick took the glass. 'Everything all right with you, Elias? Still making a lot of money?'

'Enough. How 'bout you? Only a couple of days to go now.'

'Thank God. This is my first stop then I'm off to walk round the rest of the district, so no one forgets I'm in charge. After that I'll go back to the jailhouse and relieve Dave for the night.' He sighed. 'I'll be glad when this business is over. I'm getting stiff and tired from trying to sleep at my desk.'

'Can't you sleep in one of the cells?'

'I did that once, but Hennessey did nothing but moan all night about how unfair everything was.'

'Yeah, he would.'

Kirkpatrick finished his beer. 'Best be off.'

'Be seeing you, Ralph, take care.'

'I will. You too.'

B-O-O-M!

6

'Run!' Frank yelled.

He and Jack took to their heels.

They hadn't got far when the dynamite exploded. The force of the explosion threw them up into the air and brought them down to earth with a thump. They lay, stunned, as wood and chunks of adobe fell to the ground all around them.

When they recovered and once the noise had died away, they saw that nothing was left of the dry goods store except for a pit of debris while flames and smoke filled the sky.

'Whooee!' Jack said, finding he'd got his hearing back. 'I think you done used too much dynamite.'

Frank staggered to his feet, his ears ringing, and pulled Jack up. 'Quick! Before anyone comes.'

* * *

The force and furious noise of the explosion shook every building in Felicidad.

In The Silver Dollar it shattered some of the glasses behind the bar and knocked Ned Wilkes off his feet. In alarm everyone and everything came to a halt. And when the last echoes of the blast died away they were followed by a long moment of eerie silence before all the men started talking and exclaiming.

'What the hell was that?' Pitt let go of the bar he'd been clinging to. 'You OK, Ned?' he added, as the saloon-owner scrambled to his feet, swaying a little, his face shocked and frightened.

'It's Hennessey,' Kirkpatrick said, recovering from his surprise.

'An escape attempt?'

'What else? Come on, Elias, let's find out.' The marshal began to push his way through the still startled crowd towards the swing doors.

Pitt didn't hesitate. He wasn't a

lawman and this was nothing to do with him, but Kirkpatrick needed his help. And, like everyone else in Felicidad, he had no desire to see Hennessey escape. And, like everyone else, he was also curious to discover what had happened.

When Elias and Kirkpatrick hurried out into the street they were followed by most of The Silver Dollar's customers. Already men and girls were pouring out of the other saloons and brothels. They all stopped on the street looking towards Felicidad's plaza where a pall of black smoke rose up into the air.

Shouts and cries were going up all around Kirkpatrick and Pitt.

'What is it?'

'What's wrong?'

'Let's see,' Kirkpatrick said. And, followed by what seemed like the whole of Felicidad, he raced towards the scene of the explosion.

★ ★ ★

As the O'Connors got near the marshal's office a shaken Dave Vaughan appeared in the doorway. He looked undecided as to whether to try and discover what the explosion meant or stay at the jailhouse and guard Hennessey. When he saw the two men, guns already drawn, racing towards him, his face reflected a flash of fear and he swung round to hurry back inside.

Frank was too quick for him. Even as Vaughan was pushing the door shut he fired his gun and shot the deputy. The bullet struck Vaughan between the shoulderblades and with a little groan he crashed to the floor. Callously Frank shot him again and, as Jack came into the office behind him, kicked the body to one side.

Jack slammed the door shut and holstering his gun, said, 'No one saw us, did they?' He sounded excited and was hopping from one foot to the other.

'Don't think so. But they'll guess it's got something to do with Bernie so we'd best hurry. Where are the damn keys to the cells? Stop behaving like a damn fool and help me look for 'em.'

Jack reached into the top drawer of the marshal's desk and pulled out a bunch of keys on an iron ring. 'Here.' He threw them across to Frank.

★　★　★

'Look!' Pitt pointed as they all reached the plaza. 'Oh my God.'

Mr Toombs's dry goods store had disappeared. Where it had once stood was now a gaping hole. Smoke billowed out from the wreckage and filled the sky.

Kirkpatrick's eyes searched the crowd looking for the store-owner. 'I hope Mr Toombs wasn't working late this evening.'

'There's nothing anyone can do for him if he was,' Pitt said. 'If he was in the store when it blew up he wouldn't have stood a chance.'

★　★　★

As Frank opened the door through to the cells they heard Hennessey shouting.

'What the hell is goin' on? Who is it?'

Frank grinned at Jack. 'Hey, Bernie, it's us. We're here to get you out just like we done said we would.'

Relief crossed Hennessey's face which he quickly turned into a scowl. He didn't want the O'Connors guessing how afraid he'd been that they wouldn't pull off this rescue and he'd be left to hang. He'd always found that the best way to assume control, and keep it, was to make others afraid of him; even those who were out to help him and were also family.

''Bout time,' he snarled. 'I was starting to think you'd forgotten me.'

'As if we could.' Frank was trying to fit a key into the lock.

'Hurry it up for Chris'sakes.'

'Don't know which damn key . . . ah, that's it.' The door swung open. 'C'mon, Bernie, we've got some horses waiting.'

Hennessey shoved past the two brothers. 'Let me get a gun.' He smashed open the glass-front of the gun cabinet and pulled out a rifle and a revolver as well as ammunition for both. He loaded a bullet in the breech of the Colt and pointed the weapon at Vaughan.

'He's dead, don't bother.' Jack crossed over to the door and eased it open slightly to peer out. 'And we don't want no noise alerting the good folk of Felicidad to what we're doin'.'

Hennessey didn't like being given orders and he opened his mouth to object but before he could do so Jack went on, 'People are already gathering up yonder.'

With that Hennessey saw the sense of what the other man said. Now he was out of the cell he could taste freedom; could taste revenge. He didn't intend to let anything get in the way of either. Without another word he followed the brothers out onto the sidewalk and quickly round the side of the jailhouse to where they were out of sight of the plaza. The three horses the O'Connors had stolen, stood there, waiting, saddled and bridled.

Frank unhitched them but before they could mount up Hennessey caught hold of his arm. 'Hold on.'

'What is it?'

'There's a coupla people I wanna get even with before I leave this goddamned town behind.'

'We ain't got time,' Frank protested.

'It won't take long. So make damn time.'

'You ain't goin' after the lawman are you?'

'Not yet.' Hennessey smirked evilly. He wasn't that stupid, especially as Kirkpatrick wouldn't be alone.

Frank and Jack glanced at one another. In that moment they both wondered if they'd made a mistake in rescuing Old Man Hennessey. He was already calling the shots, getting them to take unnecessary risks. But, as they were scared of him, especially when he was in one of his frequent moods, and as they needed his help, they felt they had little choice but to follow him.

★ ★ ★

At the site of the explosion Kirkpatrick quickly took charge. He turned to a couple of men behind him.

'Get others! Find some buckets, there'll be some over in the hardware store, and set up a chain for water. Make sure the fire don't spread.'

They rushed to do as he bid.

'We'd better get on down to the jail.' For the first time Kirkpatrick looked in the direction of his office, fully expecting to see that the building had also been blown up. To his surprise it was untouched. Looked quiet. No sight nor sound of anyone.

'Ralph, I don't like this,' Pitt said, as, followed by several others, they started down the road.

'Me neither.' Kirkpatrick's heart was beating wildly.

It was even worse than either man feared.

As the marshal pushed open the door the first thing he saw was Dave Vaughan laying face down on the floor, the back of his shirt soaked with blood.

'Oh God.'

While Kirkpatrick hurried through the door to the cells, Pitt went over to the deputy and turned him over. 'He's dead,' he announced grimly.

'And Hennessey has gone. Oh hell! The sonofabitch had someone here in Felicidad willing to break him out. And now a good man just doing his job is dead. I should've been the one here guarding Hennessey, not Dave.'

'It weren't your fault,' someone else said.

Pitt added, 'There were so many people in town you couldn't possibly keep an eye on them all.'

Kirkpatrick knew the others were right but that didn't make him feel any better. But there was no time to indulge in guilt. 'I'd best form up a posse and start after Hennessey.'

'I'll come with you,' Pitt said.

'Me too.' Several others clamoured for attention.

Kirkpatrick knew there would be no shortage of volunteers. They would surely pick up the trail and catch Hennessey before he got too far.

But all at once everything changed. The door was flung open and an out of breath Ned Wilkes charged in.

'Marshal,' he panted, trying to get his breath back. His words came out in little gasps. 'Three men. Hennessey's one of 'em. Riding towards Mrs Barron's boarding-house.'

'Oh my God.' There was fear in Kirkpatrick's face and voice. He turned to Pitt. 'He's going after Thora.'

'And Lizzie.'

7

Mrs Barron was busy serving the evening meal. She had just brought in a large tureen of tomato soup, when the explosion occurred. She screamed, as did Thora and Lizzie, and dropped the bowl, which shattered, the soup splashing over the carpet and furniture. While Lizzie joined the other boarders in hurrying to look out of the window, Thora went to help Mrs Barron. She bent down and started picking up the broken shards of crockery.

'What was that? What's happened?' Mrs Barron's hand went to her heart.

Thora looked over her shoulder at Lizzie. 'Can you see anything?'

'No, Miss Dowling, 'cept there's an awful lot of smoke coming from the direction of the plaza.'

'Mrs Barron, are you all right?'

'Yes, of course.' The woman had

quickly recovered from her shock. 'I heard much louder bangs during the Civil War. It took me by surprise that's all. Oh, look at the mess!' She surveyed the spilt soup in dismay. 'Whatever could have caused such a terrible noise?'

'I think something must've been blown up,' one of the boarders said.

'Was it done on purpose?' Thora asked.

The boarder shrugged. 'Let's go and find out.' He led the others towards the door.

'Lizzie, wait for me.' Thora stood up.

'Where are you two going?' Mrs Barron demanded.

'To see what's happened.' Thora was surprised at the question.

'No, don't go out there. Either of you.'

'Why not? Ralph might be involved,' Thora protested. She wanted to make sure he was all right.

'So might Mr Pitt.'

'No,' Mrs Barron repeated. 'Think of

what this could mean.' Both girls stopped to look at her. 'Mightn't it be to do with Old Man Hennessey? Perhaps someone has blown up the jail trying to get him out. Even worse they might have succeeded. He could be at large.'

'Oh.' The blood drained from Lizzie's face and she sat down abruptly as if her legs would no longer support her.

'But Ralph could be hurt . . . '

'And so could you. Thora, dear, you don't know Hennessey the way the rest of us do. He won't take kindly to anyone who has dared stand up against him. And that includes you. He'll want to take revenge on you if he can. Lizzie too, it wouldn't surprise me. Isn't that right, Lizzie?'

The girl nodded wordlessly, tears appearing in the corners of her eyes.

'You two stay here where you'll be safe. I'll go to the plaza.'

'All right,' Thora agreed reluctantly. 'You will come back straightaway, won't you?'

'Yes, dear.'

As Mrs Barron left the room, Thora went over to Lizzie and put a comforting arm around her shoulders. 'It'll be all right. Ralph and Mr Pitt won't let anything happen to us. And Hennessey can't know where we are.' She hoped not anyway, although it was difficult to keep anything secret in a small town like this. 'Anyway Mrs Barron is probably wrong. It might not be anything to do with — '

'What's that?' Lizzie interrupted. 'I thought I heard horses.'

Thora glanced towards the window. As she did so they both heard the front door crash back on its hinges and Mrs Barron let out a startled, frightened cry.

'Oh no!' Lizzie whispered. 'It's him.'

'Where the hell are they? I've come for 'em both.'

Thora shuddered. She would recognize that voice anywhere: Old Man Hennessey. Lizzie clutched Thora's hand so tightly the girl grimaced with pain.

'Get out! Go away!' That was Mrs Barron. 'I don't know what you're talking about.'

'Out of my way.'

'No! Stop!' There was a slight pause then Mrs Barron's voice rose in fear. 'Oh no, please!'

This was quickly followed by a shot, a cry and the fall of a body.

Thora felt her worst nightmare was coming true. And that she was reliving those terrible moments when Hennessey had shot and murdered three men at Freeman's stagecoach station. But this was happening now and it was far far worse. She hadn't known those men. She did know Mrs Barron. Since her arrival in Felicidad the woman had been kind to her and Thora liked her very much. Now it seemed she too had been shot, was perhaps dead. Just for trying to help her and Lizzie.

'We must hide!' she said.

But she didn't think it would do any good and before either girl could even move the door opened and a scruffy man neither of them had ever seen before peered in.

He grinned revealing blackened teeth. 'Here they are.' Behind him appeared a plumpish man. And then Old Man Hennessey.

Lizzie let out a little cry and shrank back.

Somehow Thora overcame her fear to say, 'What have you done to Mrs Barron? Is she dead?' Her voice was high and tremulous.

None of the men answered her. Instead Hennessey sauntered in like the bully that he was, closely followed by the other two.

'What now?' Frank O'Connor asked, not sounding or looking particularly pleased.

He didn't like this. It wasn't that he particularly disapproved of hurting or frightening women, although it wasn't something he'd ever done, but he wanted to be on his way before the law caught up with them. He and Jack had taken risks in coming to Felicidad and using dynamite to blow up a building. They could have been free and clear by now, instead they were still in town because of Hennessey's crazy schemes.

'They hurt me and mine and I'm goin' to punish the pair of 'em.' Hennessey glared at Thora and Lizzie and laughed loudly at the fear in their eyes. 'Like I'm goin' to punish the whole damn town.'

'We ain't got time for any of that,' Frank objected. 'We've gotta get away.'

'I ain't leaving without hurting those that hurt me,' Hennessey said stubbornly.

'Frank's right.' Jack was bouncing about with impatience. 'Someone might've heard you shoot that woman out there. Others probably saw us riding this way. C'mon, Bernie, the thing now is to get away. After all, you can always come back later when everything has done quietened down.'

'Then we take these two with us.'

'No!' Lizzie screamed. 'Please, please don't.'

'OK,' Frank agreed. Anything to get away from Felicidad.

'Leave us alone,' Thora cried. As Jack reached for her she slapped his hand away.

He grabbed hold of her arms, pulling her close so she recoiled from his bad breath. 'C'mon, girly.'

Lizzie screamed again as Hennessey snatched a handful of her hair, wrenching her head back. 'Take me, Bernie, but at least leave Miss Dowling behind.'

'You both betrayed me. You know what you deserve, don't you?' And casually Hennessey slapped her. 'Know what you're getting too.'

'Please, Bernie, don't hurt me.'

Hennessey laughed.

'Stop that.' Thora struggled uselessly against her captor. 'Leave her alone.'

'Come on!' Frank yelled, finally losing his temper. 'We must go. This second.'

Lizzie's head was down, tears in her eyes and she allowed herself to be manhandled out into the hall without putting up any resistance. Thora fought as hard as she could, kicking and punching. Screaming. But against Jack's superior strength, and against his willingness to hurt her, she stood no chance.

Oh, where was Ralph? Surely he would come looking for her? Why wasn't he here?

Mrs Barron lay on the floor in the hall, blood seeping from a wound in her side, the bonnet she'd been reaching for nearby. To Thora's relief she was still breathing and to her even greater relief the three men passed by without hurting her any more. She'd been scared that with all his wild talk Hennessey might shoot the woman again just for the sake of it.

Outside three horses stood in the road.

'We need more horses,' Hennessey said.

Frank sighed. 'The girls will have to ride with us. We've gotta leave. I mean it, Bernie.'

'OK, OK. Stop your damn fussing.'

Thora dug her heels into the ground. It was no use. She was flung up on to the back of one of the horses. Quickly Jack clambered up behind her and took hold of her again. With his arms tightly around her, pinning her own arms against her sides, he kicked the horse hard. It squealed and sprang forward. Scared she would fall off and tumble to the ground, Thora no longer dared struggle. Beside her, she was aware of Lizzie riding with Hennessey, while the third man led the way down the road.

And the three men and their two helpless captives galloped out of Felicidad, with no one around to stop them.

8

As Pitt and Kirkpatrick ran towards the boarding-house, Kirkpatrick threw off the sling supporting his arm. It was awkward, made him clumsy, and he had a dread feeling that this was a situation in which he was going to need to be as fast and sure as possible.

The first thing they noticed was that Mrs Barron's front door stood open. Any faint hope that it might simply have been left that way as the boarders hurried out to discover what had happened died as soon as they went inside. One of the chairs in the hall lay on its side and Mrs Barron lay moaning beside it.

'Thora!' Kirkpatrick yelled. No reply. His heart beat so wildly he might not have heard her anyway. 'Thora, are you here?' He was shaking with fear. 'Lizzie.'

While Ned Wilkes knelt by Mrs Barron, Kirkpatrick and Pitt hurried through the house, opening doors and peering into empty rooms, calling out the names of the two girls. They became more and more apprehensive with each step, because if Thora and Lizzie were still here they would show themselves — unless they couldn't, because Hennessey had shot them as well.

'They've gone,' Pitt said, when he rejoined the marshal at the top of the stairs. He almost sounded relieved. At least they hadn't found the girls' bodies, although perhaps the alternative was nearly as bad.

'Hennessey and whoever rescued him must have taken them.' Kirkpatrick spoke bleakly, echoing Pitt's fears.

'Coming to the boarding-house instead of just riding away he risked getting caught.'

'Maybe but it'd be just like him. He wouldn't consider the consequences. All he'd want to do is hurt Thora for testifying against him and he'd likely blame Lizzie for the trouble that befell him.' Kirkpatrick ran a trembling hand over his face. 'I should have shot the bastard when I had the chance. Said he'd tried to escape while we were bringing him in. No one would have blamed me.'

'That ain't your way.'

'No. And look what's happened as a result. Hennessey has got Thora. Oh God, what will he do to her?'

Pitt, whose own stomach seemed to be twisting somersaults at the thought of Lizzie and Thora Dowling in Hennessey's grasp, tried to offer some comfort. 'At least the girls are alive. Hennessey could've shot them and then ridden away couldn't he? Instead he's taken them with him. That gives us the chance to catch up and rescue them. Don't give up, Ralph, Thora is depending on you.'

'Don't you think I know that?' But Kirkpatrick made himself stop thinking and act instead. Thora did need him and it would do her no good if he went to pieces.

By now they had reached the hallway again where Wilkes and a couple of women neighbours were tending to Mrs Barron. The woman was conscious and sitting up, although she was white-faced with pain. Blood stained her apron and she was holding her side.

Wilkes got to his feet. 'Hennessey, the bastard, shot her when she tried to stop him coming in. That sonofabitch. He could just have easily knocked her down. Instead he deliberately shot her. She says there were two men, strangers she's never seen before, with him.'

'Will she recover?' Kirkpatrick asked anxiously.

Wilkes nodded. 'It looks to me as if it's just a deep graze. There's no sign of a bullet hole.'

From the floor Mrs Barron sat up a little straighter and said, 'Marshal, has Hennessey taken Miss Dowling and Lizzie?'

'I'm afraid so.'

'I tried to stop him. I couldn't.' Tears slid down the woman's cheeks.

'You did what you could. You were very brave,' Pitt told her. He turned back to Kirkpatrick. 'Ralph, what now?'

'I'm going after Thora. Straightaway. I can't wait to swear in a posse.' Kirkpatrick was already heading for the door.

'I'm coming with you,' Pitt said, in a voice that allowed for no argument. 'You can deputize me as we go along if you like.'

'That won't be necessary.' Kirkpatrick had no intention of behaving like a lawman when he caught up with Hennessey.

'God speed,' Mrs Barron called after them.

Out on the street Mr Toombs was coming their way at the head of a group of men.

'At least he's OK,' Kirkpatrick muttered.

'Marshal,' Toombs called out, stopping them. 'What are you doing? Where are you going?'

'After Hennessey.'

'What about my place?' Toombs began then stopped as he saw the look on the marshal's face and realized that something really bad — much worse than the destruction of his store — had occurred. 'Are you forming a posse?'

'There's no time,' Kirkpatrick said.

'What do you mean?'

Impatient to be on his way Kirkpatrick knew he'd have to take some time out to explain, and to ask for help. Leave instructions. He swallowed his anger. None of this was Toombs's fault and as he'd lost his livelihood he deserved an explanation.

'Look, Mr Toombs, you and the town council will have to sort things out here.'

'What do you want done?'

'You should send off telegrams to the county sheriff and to other marshals in the vicinity alerting them that Hennessey has escaped in the company of a couple of other men. And tell them to be careful because he's got two captives with him.'

'Who?'

'Miss Dowling and Lizzie.'

An outraged groan went up amongst the men. Everyone knew Thora Dowling was a respectable young woman; they liked her, she was brave, had stood up to Old Man Hennessey, while Lizzie was pretty and popular and had been hurt enough already.

'Mrs Barron has also been shot.'

Another groan.

'So try to find a doctor willing to make the journey here.' Kirkpatrick wasn't only thinking of Mrs Barron. He feared that Thora and Lizzie might need doctoring when they were rescued.

'OK.'

'And get some men to come after us too.'

Toombs nodded. 'Leave it all to me. You two be on your way. And be careful.'

'Come on, Ralph.' Pitt was anxious to get going.

Kirkpatrick laid a hand on Pitt's arm. 'Elias, you go and saddle up two horses while I fetch the things we'll need to take with us. I hope we can catch the bastards up before long but in case we can't we'll need some supplies. And plenty of ammunition.'

Pitt nodded agreement. 'I'll meet you at the livery stable.'

As he hurried away he looked up at the sky. The sun was dipping towards the horizon. It wouldn't be long before darkness fell. They must be on their way before then. Whoever had rescued Hennessey had chosen their time well.

Kirkpatrick went back to his office where the undertaker's men were looking after Vaughan's body.

This couldn't be happening, he thought desperately, keeping a grip on his emotions with difficulty, just couldn't. Only earlier that day he'd been congratulating himself on how well everything was going, thinking that Old Man Hennessey was due to hang in a couple of days' time and he was holding Thora in his arms, telling her that soon they could be married . . . now this!

Dave Vaughan was dead and Thora was in the grip of Hennessey, and two strangers about whom he knew nothing. God knew what they would do to her, and to poor little Lizzie. If they hurt either one . . . he didn't know what he would do, how he would cope. He and Pitt must catch them up. Must, before any harm came to either girl.

And when they did Kirkpatrick wasn't going to wait for any hangman. He was going to execute Hennessey himself.

With the help of a couple of townsmen, it didn't take long for him to get together some supplies and clothes, extra guns and spare ammunition.

When he reached the livery stable, Pitt had picked out two good animals, who looked built for both speed and endurance. He had also filled a couple of canteens with water. And listened to the complaints of the owner about how three horses had been stolen.

'Everything ready?' Kirkpatrick asked.

'Yeah.' Pitt swung up into the saddle. 'Which way d'you reckon they'll take?'

'They'll head for the valley and Mexico.'

'You sure?'

Kirkpatrick nodded. 'The other way just leads further into the mountains. They won't take that. Its treacherous and slow-going. And Hennessey knows Mexico, seeing as how he and the rest of his clan went there often enough to rustle cattle and prey on the people. He's stupid enough to believe that the Mexicans will welcome him with open arms and provide him with a safe place to stay just because they were too scared to do otherwise when he had the others with him.'

'Right, let's go.'

Kirkpatrick agreed. Enough time had been wasted already. Please God, he prayed as they galloped out of Felicidad, please don't let us be too late.

9

Thora was terrified. What did Old Man Hennessey intend doing to her and Lizzie? Well, she could guess! She didn't think the other two men would even try to stop him. They might want to join in.

As well as being petrified, she was riding awkwardly, being held in an uncomfortable position perched on the edge of the saddle. Her back was beginning to ache and she was afraid of falling from the horse and being trampled by its hoofs. She wasn't a good horse-woman at the best of times and now she seemed to be staying on the horse only because she was held there by the strong arms of her captor. Even worse he was pressed close to her and he smelt so bad it made her feel sick.

She knew Ralph would follow her but she was afraid he might be too late. He might even have been shot, although she comforted herself by telling herself that if that was the case Hennessey would have boasted about the fact to her.

They were still in the foothills, riding amongst the pine trees, when Hennessey came to a halt. The other two men stopped their horses to stare across at him in surprise.

'What're you doin', Bernie?' Frank asked.

'Got things to do,' Hennessey said. He pinched Lizzie hard, making her squeal in pain.

Thora looked at the terrified girl, wishing she could go to her. Was this where they were going to be raped and killed? She determined not to let Hennessey know how scared she was, although surely the man holding her could feel her trembling.

'Don't you think we oughtta get on while it's still light enough to see our way?' Frank said. 'That's why we done broke you out when we did.'

'Hell, OK, and I thank you,' Hennessey snarled, not sounding in the least bit grateful. 'But that bastard Kirkpatrick and the posse might be on our trail already.'

So Ralph was alive!

'We wanna get away without hurt we oughtta deal with 'em before they have a chance to catch up.' Hennessey sounded careless as if he believed he wouldn't have any difficulty whatsoever in dealing with the men from Felicidad. ''Course,' he added, grinning at Thora, 'the marshal could still be in Felicidad, still swearing in a posse, seeing as how he's always so particular 'bout following the damn law.'

Thora allowed herself a little smile. Hennessey was wrong. Ralph would be coming after her as soon as possible, even if he came alone.

'We ain't gone far enough yet,' Frank dared contradict the Old Man. 'We ain't even reached the valley.'

'Hell, I wanna shoot Kirkpatrick.' Hennessey's eyes glittered with rage and hate and he laughed as he heard Thora's gasp of distress. 'I can do that here better'n in the valley. I owe that bastard. He shot my boy dead. I should've got him back in Felicidad, not let you two order me to ride outa town like I was damn scared, which I ain't and never was. Once he's shot the rest of the damn cowards with him'll give up, leaving us free and clear. And then we can head for Mexico.'

A glance and a grimace passed between the brothers.

'What?' Hennessey demanded angrily. 'What ain't you two telling me?'

'We ain't goin' to Mexico,' Frank admitted.

'Why the hell not? Where d'you imagine we're goin' then?'

'Arizona.'

'Why? What the hell is in Arizona 'cept lawmen looking out for us? C'mon, Frank, spit it out.'

'There's a job me and Jack wanna do.'

'So go ahead and do it.'

'We need your help.'

Hennessey's eyes narrowed dangerously. 'So that's why you broke me outa jail. And there was me thinking you did it because we're kin and you wanted to help me.'

Frank could tell from Hennessey's scowl and rising voice that the man was rapidly losing his temper, something he did easily and regularly. And that he might well take it into his head to shoot both him and Jack.

'We'd've helped you anyway, Bernie, 'course we would. We was already on our way to the ranch to tell you 'bout the job when we heard 'bout your trouble. Ain't that right, Jack?'

His brother nodded.

'So where the hell does this job come in?'

'When we learnt 'bout it we thought, yeah, we'll do it! And we thought of you and knew you'd wanna be in on it 'cos if we pull it off it means a helluva lot of money for all of us.'

'Iffen I'm goin' along with you and

not riding for Mexico it'd better be worth it.'

'Oh it will,' Jack added.

'So what is it? Tell me.'

'We ain't got time for all that right now.' Frank sounded exasperated. 'We've gotta get on. So let's find some place we can watch from to see if a posse is on our trail and set up an ambush if so.'

'Think that's a good idea?' Jack asked.

Frank shrugged. He would have preferred to ride further, but ambushing the marshal was something Hennessey was intent on doing. And it had to be done quickly before it got too dark or before the posse got too close.

'Don't matter what he thinks,' Hennessey said nastily. 'It's what *I* think's important and I wanna shoot that bastard, Kirkpatrick. Up ahead there's a stand of rocks. Be a good spot to wait and watch for a while. If there ain't no sign of a posse we can go on. If there is I shoot the marshal and anyone else I can get in my sights too. I'll bag me some of the bastards for sure.'

'You can't do this,' Thora said, but no one took any notice of her.

The rocks Hennessey meant were situated near the ridge of the next hill with a good view along their backtrail. It didn't take long to reach them. When they did Jack pushed Thora to the ground. Stiff and awkward she almost fell, making the men laugh. The three men dismounted and Hennessey pulled Lizzie after him, giving her a shove that sent her sprawling. He kicked her in passing.

'You stay here,' Frank said to Jack. 'Keep an eye on them two. I'll go with Bernie.'

'OK,' Jack agreed with a little shrug. He obviously didn't like this delay any more than his brother. He pointed a finger at Thora. 'You gals don't cause me no trouble and I'll leave you be.'

Ignoring him, Thora hurried over to Lizzie, helping her up.

'Oh, Miss Dowling.' Lizzie burst into tears. 'I'm so afraid. Bernie'll kill us.'

'Ralph won't let that happen.' Thora put her arms around the girl, hugging her close.

'But you heard Bernie. He's going to shoot him.'

Thora's heart seemed to skip several beats with fear but she tried to smile. 'You shouldn't accept everything Hennessey says as fact. He's not some super being who's always right. And Ralph is hard to kill. Anyway even if he is . . . hurt, Hennessey's wrong if he believes the rest of the posse will let him get away. Mr Pitt certainly won't, will he? Come on, Lizzie dear, you must be strong.'

But Thora wondered if she could be strong herself, especially if anything did happen to Ralph. She stared up at the rocks where Hennessey and the man called Frank had almost reached the top. Could she do anything to warn Ralph? Perhaps attack Jack, grab his gun, fire off a shot . . . even as she made a move in the man's direction he turned round and grinned, almost as if he knew what she was thinking.

Lizzie said, 'Please, Miss Dowling, don't.' She caught hold of Thora's arm. 'You'll be killed and I'll be left all alone. I need you. Please don't.'

With a little sigh of defeat Thora led Lizzie over to the base of the rocks and they sat down on the dusty earth, close together. Lizzie looked too frightened to even cry any more. Thora glanced at Jack. He'd gone back to seeing to the horses. Quickly she drew a handkerchief from the pocket of her skirt. She tore off one of the corners and put it on the ground with a stone over it to keep it in place, and next to it she drew an 'A' in the earth. That might help the posse track them and at least hopefully alert them to the fact that Hennessey was headed for Arizona, not Mexico.

Oh, what was happening? Please Ralph, she prayed, please be careful.

Up near the top of the rocks, Frank suddenly gave a cry. 'There! Look!' He pointed along the way they had come to where a rising of dust was clearly visible. 'Is it them? Don't look like many riders.'

'It must be. Who else could it be?' Hennessey was scornful. 'Bet what's happened is that Kirkpatrick couldn't get none of the spineless bastards to ride with him.' He laughed. 'I made certain sure all them good townsfolk were scared of me and my kids. They probably wouldn't be eager to help a damn Easterner either.'

Whoever it was, however many, the riders were coming fast. Might have caught them up before they were out of the foothills. So, Frank thought, perhaps Hennessey was right and an ambush was the best way to deal with them; to stop the pursuit.

'Here they come!' he cried, spotting the riders through the trees on the opposite slope. 'Just two of 'em.'

Frank was surprised about that. Despite what Hennessey said, in his experience, townsmen were always willing to join posses and give chase. There was safety in numbers and he felt sure the men from Felicidad would be eager to follow Hennessey and his rescuers. Perhaps, he thought, it was because the marshal was coming fast after his 'betrothed', whom Bernie had insisted on kidnapping. Oh well, perhaps it was working out OK: two men were easier to deal with than a whole posse of infuriated citizens.

'One's Kirkpatrick. I'd recognize that bastard anywhere. The other 'un looks like that gambler, Pitt, who helped him kill my kids.' Hennessey raised his rifle.

'Wait,' Frank began. He was going to tell Hennessey to let the two men get closer so there was a clear shot. He didn't have the chance.

Hennessey was in a rage. Even as Frank spoke, before he was given time to draw his own gun let alone aim it, the other man squeezed the trigger.

After a second or two Kirkpatrick's horse reared and the marshal fell back out of his saddle.

'Yeah, got him!' Hennessey yelled in triumph.

Frank hid a disgruntled sigh. It was now too late to shoot the second man. He'd thrown himself off the horse and on to the ground and no longer presented a target. But perhaps it didn't matter. Even if the other man, a gambler, did decide to come after them, which was unlikely, he'd be delayed for a while. They were at liberty to head for Arizona and commit the perfect robbery.

Below Thora jumped as she heard the shot and her heart sank when it was followed by Hennessey's cry. Oh no, she thought, Ralph was shot, hurt, might be dead. She should have done something to warn him even if by doing so she risked her own life. Because now if Ralph was dead her life meant nothing anyway. Oh, what was she going to do? Beside her, Lizzie started to cry, but however heartbroken Thora was she would never, ever, do anything to let Hennessey know.

10

The shot came out of nowhere, without warning.

It hadn't taken Pitt and Kirkpatrick long to pick up the trail of the three horses. They had been ridden fast along the road out of town and Hennessey and his rescuers hadn't tried to hide their tracks; their only intent was escape. The trail was easy to see and easy to follow, which was lucky as Pitt and Kirkpatrick were only intent on catching them up.

As they topped a ridge, Kirkpatrick pointed ahead. He slowed his horse slightly and called across to Pitt. 'That's their dust. If we don't catch them in the hills we should do so once we reach the valley.'

'We need to be careful,' Pitt warned. 'If they spot us they might hurt the girls so they can get away.' He couldn't quite bring himself to use the word 'kill', but he didn't doubt that Hennessey would be only too capable of killing defenceless young women if it suited his purpose.

If Kirkpatrick's anxious face was anything to go by he believed the same. 'Even a fool like Hennessey must realize I'll be chasing after him but perhaps he might think it'll take some time for me to form a posse. Hopefully none of them will guess we're so close behind.'

'Perhaps not.'

And that was when Old Man Hennessey fired his rifle. The bullet whined by the ear of Kirkpatrick's horse and caused it to rear in fright. Taken by surprise, Kirkpatrick tumbled out of the saddle and the horse galloped away before coming to a stop halfway down the hill.

'Goddammit!' Pitt swore and dragged his own horse to a halt. He flung himself to the ground and clawed out his gun, lifting his head slightly to stare across at the boulders from where the rifle-shot had come. Heart thumping he waited. Nothing happened. There were no more shots.

He glanced across at Kirkpatrick. With a sinking feeling he saw that the man still lay where he had fallen. Was he badly hurt? Don't say he was dead!

After a couple more minutes, Pitt got to his feet, prepared to dive back down to the ground if he was shot at. Again nothing happened. Keeping low, he hurried over to the marshal. At first he couldn't see any blood but as he got closer he realized the man's shirt was reddening all down his left arm.

'Ralph, Ralph, you OK?'

Kirkpatrick stirred. His eyes blinked open and disorientated he tried to sit up, then with a groan flopped back down. He raised a hand to his head. 'What is it?'

'Someone fired at us and you fell off your horse. You've been shot.'

'I don't think so.'

'There's blood everywhere.'

A little shakily Kirkpatrick looked down at his arm and reached under his shirt. 'Hell, the wound has opened up. That's all.'

It was enough.

'Did you break anything when you landed on the ground? You landed with a thump.'

'Help me up.' Kirkpatrick got to his feet and gingerly tested his legs by putting his full weight on them. He grimaced as his back gave a painful twinge. 'No, nothing's broken. What about you?'

'I'm OK. You all right to go on?'

'Of course.' Kirkpatrick sounded surprised that Pitt had asked the question.

But as he still looked white and shaken, Pitt said, 'Even so you'd better sit down for a while, rest up, and I'll see to your arm.'

'There's no time.'

'Yeah, there is.'

Kirkpatrick opened his mouth to protest but even as he did so his senses swirled and he swayed a little. 'Perhaps you're right.' He collapsed on the ground.

'I'll get your horse.'

Pitt started down the hillside after the animal. As he did so he spotted a rise of dust in the air on the trail below. Hennessey and the others were on the move again. And he and Kirkpatrick were stuck here for a while. Damn!

The horse was still nervous and although he spoke quietly to it, it skittered away from him. Eventually it stood still long enough for him to grab hold of the reins and once he had done so it followed him back to where Kirkpatrick waited without further bother. He was thankful to see that the marshal looked slightly better.

'Here, Elias, you can use this to bind my arm. It's clean.' Kirkpatrick had taken off his bandanna and he handed it over.

Pitt wet his own bandanna with water from the canteen and wiped away the blood on Kirkpatrick's arm and shoulder as best he could. Then he wrapped the clean bandanna around the wound and tied it tightly. 'That comfortable?'

'Yeah.' Kirkpatrick spoke impatiently, obviously not caring how uncomfortable the bandage was or if he was in pain. All he could think of was that Hennessey was probably miles ahead by now. 'Let's go.' He was anxious to get on his way.

Pitt paused, looking up at the sky. It would soon be full dark, especially amongst the trees.

'We'll have to stop for the night before long,' he said, although he felt sure Kirkpatrick wouldn't like it and before the man could object, went on, 'It's stupid to ride any further when we can't follow their trail. I know you believe Hennessey will go to Mexico but you don't know that for certain. If we ride there and you're wrong we might never pick up the trail again. You don't want to lose 'em, do you?'

'No!'

'And we can't take a chance on one of the horses getting hurt. Anyway Hennessey will probably have to stop as well.'

'All right,' Kirkpatrick agreed with a scowl. 'Just a bit further though. At least let's get to the rocks where that shot came from.'

It was dark and turning cold when they got there.

'Look, Elias, the girls sat down over here by themselves. No one went near them.' Kirkpatrick breathed an inward sigh of relief. He had been dreading that he would find some evidence of Thora having been attacked. 'What's this?' He bent down.

'What is it?'

'A piece of Thora's handkerchief caught up under a stone.' Kirkpatrick smiled. 'Clever girl. She's leaving us a trail to follow.'

'What's that by it?' Pitt pointed to the ground. 'Watch where you're stepping! There, see. It looks like something has been written in the dirt.'

Kirkpatrick pushed his hat back on his head. 'You're right. It's an A. Thora must have written that. A? What can that mean?'

'One of the men has a name beginning with A?' Pitt hazarded a guess.

'Maybe,' Kirkpatrick agreed. 'She must believe it's important.' He wished he knew what Thora had been trying to tell him; if he thought hard enough he might work it out. 'Perhaps she'll be able to leave us further clues as we go on. She'll try anyway.' He smiled again.

Pitt looked round. 'This is as good a place as any to stop.'

'OK. Best not risk a fire. Hennessey probably believes he shot and killed me and that he's now safe from pursuit. That gives us an edge.'

Pitt nodded agreement. It would be a long, freezing night, without even a mug of coffee to warm them but Kirkpatrick was right. And the safety of Thora and Lizzie, their rescue, was more important than his and Ralph's comfort.

As they settled down to eat some cold rations, Kirkpatrick found he wasn't hungry anyway. His arm was hurting and so was his back where he'd fallen off the horse but he was determined to ignore both. Nothing was going to stop him following Thora.

After a moment or two of silence, Pitt said, 'I wonder if Mr Toombs succeeded in getting a posse together?'

'There'll be men eager to join it.' Kirkpatrick frowned. 'But by the time Toombs sent out those telegrams I asked him to, and then there was Dave's body to attend to, it'd be dark. I don't reckon they'll start out till tomorrow morning at the earliest.'

'Me neither. Guess we're on our own.'

'For now anyway. God, Elias, I can't believe Dave Vaughan is dead. He was a good man. Reliable. He made it clear he never wanted to be any more than a deputy and he helped me a lot when I was first appointed marshal.'

'What happened wasn't your fault.'

'I know, but I can't help but think there was something I could or should have done.'

'I don't see what.'

Nor did Kirkpatrick, not really.

'Ralph, who d'you think the men are who got the Old Man out of jail?'

'God knows.' Kirkpatrick shrugged and winced. 'That's the trouble, it could be anyone. According to local talk the Hennesseys had relatives in various parts of the country. Or it might be a couple of outlaws who found refuge at their ranch at one time or another.'

And they had hold of Thora, and Lizzie.

He stood up and looked down the road even though he couldn't see very far along it. Anything could be happening to Thora and Lizzie right then. Anything. And he and Pitt were stuck here far away and couldn't help them.

11

Not that anything was happening, at least not to Thora.

When they came to the edge of the foothills, still amongst the pine trees but with the vast empty valley before them, Frank decided they must make camp for the night.

'We won't find any shelter once we hit the desert,' he said. 'Look out for somewhere, OK?'

Jack agreed.

Hennessey smiled. 'Then when we stop I can deal with these two.' And he gave Thora an evil grin.

Despite her intentions not to show fear she shrank back against Jack.

Before long they came to a small clearing just off the road that the two brothers felt provided a good campsite.

Thora didn't know if she was relieved they'd stopped because her body ached so much, or terrified of what might happen now.

Although she knew it was useless to think she could fight the men off, Thora was prepared to die defending her honour. In the event, to her surprised relief, neither Frank nor Jack even tried to touch her.

Instead after Hennessey had taken Lizzie away to vent some of his fury on her, they huddled together by the camp-fire talking and glancing round. There was much sighing and eye rolling and Thora had the feeling that they weren't happy, that things perhaps weren't going in the way they'd planned. Not that she dared hope this would make any difference to her or Lizzie's situation. These men might be wishing they hadn't rescued Old Man Hennessey, but they wouldn't go up against him for the sake of two young women they didn't know and didn't care about.

Thora feared Hennessey would want to do the same to her as he was doing to Lizzie. But when he came back to the camp, Lizzie following on behind him with downcast eyes and refusing to look at anyone or anything, he'd taken no notice of Thora. Instead he sat down and ate some food, which he pronounced as disgusting, drank some coffee, which evidently wasn't much better, then said, 'Make sure you tie them two little gals up, don't want 'em getting away from me.' After which he rolled up into a saddle blanket and went to sleep.

Thora thought that maybe he felt having shot and killed Ralph Kirkpatrick was punishment enough for her, for the moment anyway, or maybe he was plain tired out from the hard ride. Lizzie came over to her and Thora gave her a quick hug before they were dragged apart so Jack could tie their hands behind their backs, which he did with quick efficiency.

'Don't we get a blanket?' Thora asked. 'It's cold.'

'Don't push your luck,' Jack told her,

but all the same he came back to throw a saddle blanket over them.

Once the men had settled down for the night and were asleep and snoring loudly, Thora rolled over to be close to Lizzie. The girl was crying bitterly, one eye already blackening and her cheek bruised where Hennessey had hit her, while her shirt was torn at the shoulder.

'Be brave, Lizzie, we'll get out of this somehow.'

'How?'

Thora didn't know how to answer the girl. 'Let's cuddle up together. Keep warm.'

Huddled with Lizzie under the blanket but still frozen, her toes and fingers almost numb, and uncomfortable with her hands tied behind her, Thora lay awake long into the night. She was unable to sleep, wondering what tomorrow would bring and knowing that if Ralph was dead she didn't much care.

★ ★ ★

Pitt and Kirkpatrick were awake and ready to ride as soon as light streaked the eastern sky.

Kirkpatrick felt stiff and sore. His shoulder ached and so did his back. He just hoped that moving about would ease out the kinks but if not he'd just have to live with them.

They found the clearing in which Hennessey and the others had made camp but of course they had long gone. After that it was only a matter of minutes before they emerged from the hills into the duncoloured valley that led all the way to Mexico.

Knowing Kirkpatrick was in pain, Pitt got off his horse to inspect the tracks for him.

'They still following the trail?'

'Yeah.'

'Eventually they'll come to Freeman's stage station and then it'll only be a short distance to the border.'

'What happens if they cross into Mexico before we catch up?'

'We cross after them.'

'OK.'

Since Hennessey had shot Clint Freeman and Jamie, the young helper, the stage station had stood empty, although Wells Fargo were anxious that it be reopened to handle their coaches that ran from Lordsburg to Nogales.

And it was here where the well-travelled trail divided into three directions — to Mexico, to Lordsburg, and to Nogales — that it was no longer possible to pick out Hennessey's tracks.

Kirkpatrick dismounted and walked round, feeling better now he'd been riding for a while and with the sun warm on his body.

Pitt led both horses over to a water-trough that still had a little water left in it and took the opportunity to fill up the canteens as well. 'Do we ride for Mexico?'

Kirkpatrick frowned. 'I've been thinking about that A Thora wrote in the sand. It can't be anything to do with a man's name. If it did she'd know it wouldn't mean anything to me way out here where I can't look at any wanted posters. You know, Elias, I think she was trying to tell me they were headed for Arizona, not Mexico.'

'Are you sure? You thought they were going to Mexico.'

'I know and, no, I'm not absolutely sure. But me and Thora grew up together. We were good friends before we fell in love. We think alike and we know the way each other's minds work.'

Pitt had never been that close to any girl but he supposed Kirkpatrick could be right. 'So what do you want to do?'

'Let's ride along the stageroad towards Arizona for a while. If we don't come across their tracks soon we can come back here and search the other two roads.' Kirkpatrick hoped it wouldn't come to that as it would waste too much time.

And, thank God, before they had gone very far Pitt's sharp eyes spotted something: a piece of white fluttering under a stone. Kirkpatrick's heart skipped a beat. Was it a piece of Thora's handkerchief?

He dismounted and went over to it. Yes it was!

'Thora's still pointing the way she and Lizzie are being taken,' he said, feeling so proud of her. However scared, however hurt, she was using her head, trying to help him.

Pitt had ridden on a short way and now he stopped to beckon Kirkpatrick to him. 'And, look, Ralph, here are their tracks.'

'How do you know it's them?'

'I noticed that just before we reached Freeman's one of the horses had chipped a bit from its front hoof on the right side.'

'Good. That'll make the tracks easy to follow. Let's go.'

'What about any posse following on behind us?' Pitt asked, leaning across his saddlehorn. 'Will they realize we've come this way? Or should we go back to Freeman's and make our trail clear?'

Kirkpatrick paused. 'We haven't time

to do that. We'll just have to hope for the best. Is that OK with you?'

Pitt nodded agreement. 'Yeah. We don't even know if there is a posse and if there is it'll be quite a way behind us anyway.' Might not catch up by the time they hopefully caught up with Hennessey.

'I don't know this route, do you?' Kirkpatrick asked as they rode on.

'Not well.' Pitt tried to avoid the heat of the desert country so near to Mexico if possible. 'I have ridden part of it a couple of times but that was some years ago now. The thing we'll have to watch out for is whether they continue on the Nogales road or take the turn off for Tucson. But that's still a good way ahead. I don't remember any other route they can take.'

His gaze scoured the country: the vast, empty and hot desert. If for some reason their quarry didn't keep to the stagecoach road their tracks would be easy to spot.

12

Mr Toombs sat behind Kirkpatrick's desk in the marshal's office. He was fretting over what he would do now that his store and his livelihood were in ruins. He couldn't rebuild the place because there was hardly anything left: just a pile of rubble and pieces of charred wood. The other members of the town council had promised him help but hadn't yet said when that would be forthcoming or what form it would take.

As the door opened and Ned Wilkes came in he put his worries to one side and even did his best to smile a greeting. There were after all two young women in a much worse situation than he was.

'The last reply to your telegraph messages has come,' Wilkes said, waving a piece of paper at Toombs.

'Any luck?'

'Nope. Like the rest of 'em, the marshal promises to look out for Hennessey but he ain't been spotted yet.' Wilkes sat down opposite Toombs and took off his hat, placing it on the desk. 'Still, it's early days. I doubt whether Hennessey has had time to reach any of these towns yet however hard he rides. If, that is, he heads in the direction of any of 'em. I reckon he's more likely to go to Mexico and if so now Freeman's station is no more there ain't any places or people on the way down there.'

'He could vanish into thin air,' Toombs said glumly. And if that happened Felicidad would always live with the fear of the man returning to wreak his revenge on the town.

'Marshal Kirkpatrick and Elias Pitt will do their utmost not to allow that to happen.'

'But if he crosses the border . . . ' Toombs's voice faded away. Both men knew that with Thora Dowling in Hennessey's grasp, Kirkpatrick wouldn't let a little thing like crossing an international border stop him following her. 'How's Mrs Barron this morning? Have you been to see her?'

Wilkes nodded. 'She's doing fine, thank God. She had a peaceful night's sleep. And a couple of her neighbours are looking in on her and also cooking and cleaning at the boarding-house so she doesn't lose any of her boarders. It'll take more than a slight wound to stop Mrs Barron! Oh, a doctor is on his way from Lordsburg.'

'That's two pieces of good news.' Toombs turned to bad news. 'I shall have to see the undertaker soon to make arrangements for Dave Vaughan's funeral.'

'Shouldn't we wait till Kirkpatrick gets back? He'll want to be here for that. The two of 'em got on well.'

'I know but he could be away for a while yet. Vaughan deserves to be buried and soon. I just hope the town turns out for him.'

'I'm sure they will.'

But Toombs wasn't quite so certain. He stood up and went to the window looking out on the plaza. What a change from just the previous day. Then all had been bustle and noise, now hardly anyone was abroad. A few people were shopping or going about important business but those who didn't have to be outdoors were staying inside, fearful that Old Man Hennessey, and his rescuers, would return and start shooting up the town and everyone in it. The ranchers had returned home already, scared that their lonely ranches could be on Hennessey's route. They'd taken their cowhands with them.

Not that anyone could be blamed. Everyone was upset about Miss Dowling and Lizzie being kidnapped, they were worried about the marshal and Pitt. But understandably they were mostly concerned about themselves and their families. The Hennessey clan had terrified people for so long they were still terrified.

And it made him wonder whether

many people would dare attend the deputy's funeral.

He came back to the desk and sat down again. 'I've spent the morning going through the wanted posters. From the way you and some others described the two men who rode out with Hennessey and the fact that the Old Man had a lot of relatives roundabout I reckon these are likely candidates.' He handed Wilkes a flyer.

It was headed WANTED — DEAD OR ALIVE. And went on — 'Frank and Jack O'Connor for murder committed in the course of a robbery of the Wells Fargo stage near Tucson in March of this year'. There followed a description of the two men and the offer of a reward of $200.

Toombs frowned. 'At the back of my mind I seem to remember talk of the O'Connors being distant cousins or some such of Hennessey. They came from Texas. El Paso I think.'

'Yeah, that's right. It certainly sounds like the two I glimpsed. Let's hope

Marshal Kirkpatrick realizes the part about bringing them in dead. By the way, when did the posse go out?'

'Just gone seven this morning. Finally. There were eight of 'em. A few cowboys and the rest townsmen. All young men. There would've been more if the marshal had been here to lead 'em or if they'd been after anyone else but Hennessey.' Toombs shook his head. 'I wish someone older, more responsible, had agreed to go along to keep an eye on them.' Perhaps he should have offered but it was a long while since he'd ridden a horse, he would have slowed them down. 'Or someone able to follow a trail.'

'They'll do their best. And Kirkpatrick and Pitt must've stopped for the night so hopefully the posse will catch them up before long. Then they can continue on together.'

'Yeah.'

But the two men were doomed to disappointment. The posse returned late that afternoon. Hot, covered with

106

dust, and unlucky.

'We're real sorry, Mr Toombs.' The leader was a young man who worked as a clerk in the hardware store. 'We followed the trail to Freeman's but we lost the tracks there.'

Toombs sighed in disappointment. 'Couldn't you find them again?'

'We looked all over. Honestly. Especially on the road to Mexico. But we never came across 'em again. Some of the others insisted on returning to Felicidad.' The young man sounded upset.

'The cowboys?' They would only have joined the posse in the hope of excitement and once that hope died they would quickly lose interest.

'Yeah and a couple of my friends who were anxious to get back to their families in case Hennessey showed up here. There weren't enough of us left to carry on looking. I'm sorry,' he repeated.

'It's OK, it's not your fault.' Toombs knew it was unfair to criticize him or the rest of them. They weren't lawmen and hadn't had a lawman to lead them.

'I suppose I could find some others and ride out again.' Clearly the young man was no longer enthusiastic about the idea.

'No.' Toombs shook his head. 'There's no point now.' Kirkpatrick and Pitt were alone out there and would have to take their chances.

13

It was early afternoon when the small group of four men reached the dusty streets of Tucson. It had been a long ride from the Cotton Creek mine and the two young miners with the party couldn't hide their excited joy at the thought of beer, gambling and women.

'Mr Wymark, it OK iffen we leave you here?' one of them asked. 'You'll be OK, won't you?'

'Yeah, go on.'

Archie Wymark knew the other men liked accompanying him because it meant they could spend a night in Tucson and enjoy what the town had to offer — better saloons and drink, better prostitutes than in Cotton Creek, a billiards hall, even a dance-hall. Good gambling. More action because seldom anything much happened in Cotton Creek or at the mine.

The guard with them was a new man who'd looked bored all through the ride and annoyed at having to take orders from Wymark, clearly feeling he should have been in charge. Doubtless he would also depart for the heady delights as soon as the money was counted and put in the Wells Fargo safe for collection the following morning.

Leaving Wymark — old and dull — all by himself.

'Remember,' he added, as the two miners went to ride away, 'we leave first light tomorrow. Don't be late.'

'No, Mr Wymark,' they chorused.

They looked at one another, giggling and thumping each other on the arm. The guard couldn't hide a grin at their antics. Wymark knew they were laughing at him, someone too old to enjoy the things they did.

The trouble was they were right. Wymark didn't much like Tucson. It was too noisy and crowded. Too impersonal. He preferred the quieter town of Cotton Creek where he knew everyone and liked them too. After a hard day's work at the mine, his needs were simple: a beer or two, a woman once a week, perhaps a game of poker where the bets on each hand never rose above a few cents. So while others might consider it boring, he thought of it as home, and if that made him boring as well then so be it.

The Wells Fargo office was situated in the business district. Wymark and the guard walked there once they'd left their horses at the livery. At this time of day it was empty of customers. The clerk, who knew Wymark well, looked up at the entrance of the two men and smiled.

'Afternoon,' he said. He opened the safe and drew out a heavy bag which he handed over to Wymark. 'Here you are, sir, all there I think you'll find.'

'It usually is.' Wymark emptied the money out onto the table while the guard stood in the office doorway, hand on the butt of his gun, and looked threatening.

'Just the payroll,' the clerk continued, a question in his voice.

'That's right. I'm not buying anything this trip.' Wymark finished counting the money. 'Yeah, that's it all.' He transferred the bills into four saddle-bags and handed them back to the clerk. 'Lock them up for me, please, and we'll be by to collect them early in the morning.'

'Sure thing. See you then.'

Left to his own devices the guard soon disappeared in the direction of the saloons. Wymark made his way down the street to the small hotel where he always stayed. He sighed, thinking about the lonely night ahead of him but not tempted to do as the others did.

These days he would prefer that someone else lead the group. But as assistant to Adam Fletcher, the mine's manager, part of his job was to collect the payroll once every three months. As Fletcher said, someone responsible had to go but Wymark no longer liked the responsibility. Nor the journey.

From the mine to Tucson was a couple of days' ride and hot in all seasons of the year but especially so at the beginning of summer. Unfortunately there was no other way of getting there and back; no railroad, not even a stagecoach line, although Wells Fargo kept talking about putting one in. As they'd been talking about it for years Wymark didn't hold out much hope it would happen any time soon.

And while the ride had never proved dangerous he and the others had to keep a watch out for Indians and bandits. Luckily he knew he could depend on the three men with him to shoot and kill if necessary. Wymark was willing to do the same, though he'd never yet even drawn his gun in anger, let alone shot at anyone. But he practised target shooting once a week and knew he could hit what he aimed at.

He ate dinner at a table shared with a couple of drummers and a rancher who infuriated them all with stories about how he was going to make it big, as if it would be oh so simple. He then went up to his room. The hotel didn't run to providing a bath but there was hot water in a bowl and a clean towel. After he'd washed he stretched out on the lumpy bed, thinking about things.

He'd worked for the mine for a great number of years, almost since it was opened up and, while he had been a young man back then, he was now nearing his fortieth birthday. Although he was based mostly in the mine offices the work still involved long hours and a great deal of paperwork. He was also responsible for holding negotiations between the miners and what they wanted on one side and Mr Fletcher and the owners and what they were prepared to offer on the other. More often than not this proved volatile as each group usually wanted something completely different.

And lately on these rides to Tucson, spending so much time on horseback, travelling through difficult country, his back and legs ached. He was getting too old for this way of life. The younger men considered him ancient and that was how he was beginning to feel. The work no longer seemed as interesting as it once had. It was time for a change.

So he'd decided that as soon as he did turn forty he would quit, perhaps go into partnership with Bill Temple, who owned Cotton Creek's general store. They got on well and they'd already spoken about the possibility. Temple, who was busy with so many different projects, hadn't seemed reluctant.

Wymark was also lonely. His wife had died ten years ago and he'd been alone ever since. While he would never forget her, would always love her, he felt it was time to move on and find someone else with whom to share his life. He wasn't bad-looking and he had money saved. Unfortunately at the moment there was no girl living in Cotton Creek whom he loved or wanted to marry. He supposed he might have to keep a look out for someone on these trips. Who knew? Surely it wouldn't be too difficult to meet some young lady who would appreciate him.

In the meantime there was this journey to get through.

14

It was soon obvious to Pitt and Kirkpatrick that Hennessey and his rescuers were no longer riding fast; in fact for the most part the horses were being kept to a walk, which was sensible in the heat of the afternoon. Neither were they bothering to hide their tracks.

'They must believe they're safe from pursuit,' Kirkpatrick said. 'Or else Hennessey is more stupid than I thought.'

'Well, for the moment perhaps it's best we are some way behind them. They're already becoming careless and won't be expecting us to catch up. We can take them by surprise.'

Kirkpatrick didn't share Pitt's optimism. 'But it's wild country up ahead and they can lose themselves amongst it,' he fretted. 'We might never overtake them.'

Might never rescue Thora and Lizzie, might never learn the fate of the two girls. That was his greatest fear.

Pitt could say little to comfort him, because he feared the same. It would be difficult, perhaps impossible, to follow the tracks if Hennessey's party headed into the hills. They could then go in any number of directions.

Kirkpatrick halted his horse to take a drink from his canteen. 'You know, Elias, what I still can't understand is why they're heading for Arizona and not Mexico. I felt sure that's where Hennessey would go.'

'Maybe it ain't down to him. Maybe the two men who rescued him are calling the shots.'

'Umm maybe.' Kirkpatrick sounded doubtful. 'But Hennessey was always the one in charge. I can't see him taking orders from anyone else, not even those who helped him, especially when his life might be put in danger because of it. Hennessey is stupid but he's also cunning. He must know that lawmen in

118

the area will be on the look out for him.'

Pitt wiped sweat away from his forehead and neck and squinted into the hazy distance. 'The only thing I can think of is that he was rescued not just to save him from the hangman but for a specific reason.'

'In Arizona?'

'Looks like it, don't it?'

Kirkpatrick agreed with a little nod. 'But what, I wonder? A robbery of some kind, I suppose.'

'I've been wondering about that as well. The men used dynamite to blow up Mr Toombs's store and seemed to know what they were doing. Not many men would be willing or able to handle dynamite.'

'They used more than was necessary.'

'Granted, but that might even have been done on purpose for effect. It worked anyway, didn't it, and caused enough confusion to let 'em get away? Which they might not've done if they'd just charged the jailhouse.'

Kirkpatrick agreed. The marshal's office and the jailhouse had been built to withstand attack. He would have got there before they'd managed to break the Old Man out.

'So, Ralph, where did they get the dynamite? You can't just buy it in a general store. Well, there are mines in Arizona. Silver mines mostly. And they use dynamite to blast tunnels. Couldn't these men have once been miners, or at least lived somewhere near to a mine where they could have stolen the dynamite?'

Kirkpatrick thought about that. 'Seems likely.'

'I reckon they're going back to Arizona to rob a silver mine.'

'You could be right. But which one? The problem is there are plenty of mines in the area. Some big and well guarded. Some quite small, little more than one-man jobs. Do you know of one in the immediate vicinity?'

'No.'

'Nor me. Anyway our job is to rescue

the girls. Stopping a robbery can come later. But,' Kirkpatrick added with a smile, 'whatever they're up to, Hennessey won't like it when he finds out he's being used.'

It was in the early evening when Pitt said, 'Ralph, we'll have to make camp again soon.' And when Kirkpatrick protested, he added, 'We might be able to go on but the horses certainly can't. They need to rest.'

Kirkpatrick reluctantly agreed. Travel in this heat was exhausting for the animals. And them. His old bullet wound had started to ache again, although thankfully it had stopped bleeding.

'Perhaps we can have a fire and coffee tonight as well. I don't suppose Hennessey'll be watching his back trail any longer.'

'All right.'

But if Pitt thought that a fire and hot coffee and bacon and beans would cheer up the marshal he was wrong.

Kirkpatrick lay awake nearly all

night, unable to sleep, tossing and turning, worrying.

Pitt might like Lizzie but he didn't love her. Whereas his whole body ached wanting to see Thora again, to hold her in his arms, tell her it was all right. Make sure she was all right. If anything happened to her he didn't know what he would do. Or what if she was dead? He shivered with fear. In either case he certainly wouldn't rest until he'd killed Old Man Hennessey, but that wouldn't bring Thora back. What would he do without her? What would he do if she was alive but no longer wanted anything to do with him, blaming him for her kidnap.

He'd understand her reaction because it was going to be hard to forgive himself.

He knew he'd acted selfishly in being determined to travel West to become a lawman when he could, should, have been content to be a town constable back home in Pennsylvania. It was all very well saying Thora had agreed with him, had been as excited as he was at the thought of beginning a life together away from the confines of the small town where they'd grown up. She didn't know what it was like out here. He was the one who should have known better.

Even worse he'd asked Thora to join him when he knew how dangerous it was in Felicidad with the Hennessey clan in control. He'd risked her life because he wanted her with him. And now he might have lost her forever.

As for catching up, which Pitt kept telling him they were doing . . . well, Kirkpatrick wasn't a tracker and neither was Elias so how could he tell that?

Dawn seemed an awful long way away.

15

Kirkpatrick was right. Old Man Hennessey certainly wasn't happy. He might be out of jail, escaped from the threat of the hangman, he might have his hands on Lizzie again, had punished Thora Dowling by shooting the marshal but the O'Connors were making him ride hard; they didn't have any whiskey and they were heading for Arizona. They wanted him for a job and, despite Frank's protests to the contrary, Hennessey doubted they would have broken him out of jail otherwise.

He was the one used to giving out orders and he didn't like having to do what others told him, especially when the others were the likes of Frank and Jack: idiots the pair of them!

Now he called across to Frank, 'Hey, ain't we stopping soon? It's nearly night. I'm tired and real hungry. Don't know why we've gone on so long, there ain't no pursuit. Look back and you'd damn well know that for yourself. I shot the marshal, remember? We saw him fall.'

Frank sighed. He seemed to have done a lot of sighing since rescuing Hennessey. Up ahead on the dusty trail a thick stand of cottonwoods covered the first slopes of a low ridge of hills.

'We can make camp there,' he said.

Thora was almost as glad as Hennessey when at last they came to a halt. Her whole body ached, her head pounded so hard it seemed to be splitting open and she felt she would rather die than go on any further. While she knew she should be working out ways for her and Lizzie to escape, she found she could think of nothing but how dreadful she felt. Glancing at Lizzie's face she knew the other girl was in no better state. As the men made camp they sat off to one side, holding hands, not daring to say or do anything to draw attention to themselves.

Over supper during which Hennessey complained unceasingly about the food and the coffee, he said, 'What's this damn job then? How much further we gotta go? I don't wanna ride too far from the border.'

'It's in a place called Cotton Creek.' Frank finished his coffee and put the mug on the ground.

'Never heard of it,' Hennessey growled.

'It's a small town on the way to Nogales,' Jack said. 'But further up in the hills.'

'And what's there we're goin' to rob?'

Frank glanced across at Thora and Lizzie. 'Not in front of them two.'

Hennessey laughed. 'Why not? They ain't goin' nowhere. Ain't got no one to tell now Kirkpatrick's dead. C'mon, Frank, tell me. What's at Cotton Creek?'

'There ain't much there 'cept a silver mine.' Frank spoke reluctantly.

'And we're stealing some silver from it?'

'Not 'xactly.'

'Then exactly what?' Hennessey yelled, making everyone jump. 'Hell, Frank, you sure do like your little secrets. Hell! I don't even know why I'm riding along with you two and not heading for Mexico. I could've been there by now sheltered by my friends.'

Frank thought Hennessey was living in false hope if he believed that. The Mexicans would have few reasons to welcome the man after the way he'd robbed them mercilessly for so many years. He didn't dare say so.

'We did rescue you,' Jack pointed out.

'If it comes to that I'd've escaped by my own self.'

At this Frank couldn't prevent himself from speaking up. 'You weren't making a very good job of it. There were only two days to go and the noose would've been around your neck.'

Thora thought Frank was a bit reckless talking like that.

So, obviously, did Hennessey. He leapt to his feet, flinging his mug of coffee at the man. Luckily there were only a few dregs left in the bottom and Frank wasn't splashed with any hot liquid. 'I had a damn plan.'

Frank stood up, facing Hennessey. 'And so have we. It won't take long to carry it out and after it you can go where you want. And believe me, Bernie, we'll be glad to see the back of you!'

'Not nearly as much as I wanna see the back of you two.'

'Shut up,' Jack said, before the argument could get completely out of hand, because goodness knew what would happen if it did. 'Can't we try to get along?' A whine entered his voice. 'We should help one another. We are kin.'

'And what happens to us after they've done this job?' Lizzie whispered tiredly, resting against the trunk of the tree by which she and Thora sat.

'I don't know,' Thora admitted. 'But they haven't done it yet and the way they're quarrelling perhaps they never will.'

She watched as the three men continued sniping at one another, and she wondered whether Hennessey's renowned temper would get the better of him and make him start lashing out. As long as he lashed out at Frank and Jack and not her or Lizzie she didn't really care.

Once the meal was over Jack came over to them. He tied Lizzie's hands behind her back then turned to Thora.

'Hell, Frank, I don't like any of this.' Hennessey began complaining again. 'I ain't used to all this riding around. I like my home comforts.' His voice held an ugly note and a mug clattered to the ground.

Jack was distracted and left Thora to go back and support his brother.

Soon, obviously worn out from his unaccustomed activity, Hennessey slumped down by the remains of the camp-fire and began snoring loudly. Relieved he hadn't bothered her again, Lizzie also lay down. The two brothers stayed awake a little longer but they too were now asleep.

Thora was the only one left awake. With a little leap of her heart she had realized that Jack had forgotten all about her and not tied her up properly. She thought that with a bit of luck, and persistence, she could get free of her bonds!

They could get away!

'Lizzie.' She leant forward to whisper in the other girl's ear. 'Lizzie, wake up.'

Lizzie stirred. 'What is it?'

'Jack didn't tie me up tightly. We can undo the knots.'

'Oh, Miss Dowling.'

'Sshh.' Thora glanced towards their captors who weren't far away. In fact Frank's feet were almost touching hers and she quickly drew back her legs in case he felt her moving. 'Hush, quiet. Here, help me.'

She turned her back towards Lizzie and immediately the girl reached awkwardly for the knots. Hennessey muttered in his sleep and they came to an anxious halt, looking across at him, but he didn't wake and immediately started snoring again. Before long one of the knots came loose enough for Thora to pull her hands out of the ropes.

'Quick!' She ignored the pain in her hands and arms and started to work on the ropes binding Lizzie. The girl had been tied securely and it took Thora some while to loosen the knots but she was determined not to give in and eventually she succeeded. When she had done so she hardly dared look round at the men in case they were all watching her but they weren't, they were still asleep.

'Oh, miss!' Lizzie breathed a sigh of relief as she rubbed feeling back into her hands. 'Now what?'

'We get out of here.' Slowly and carefully Thora got to her feet, helping Lizzie up after her.

'Shall we take a couple of the horses?'

Thora looked longingly at the animals but they were on the far side of the camp. To get to them would mean circling the men. She didn't think she could dare do that. Besides, the horses were unsaddled. They would never be able to saddle even one animal without making enough noise to waken their captors. And she doubted she would be able to ride barebacked. Perhaps they could free one of the horses and lead it away? What about the canteens of water? She couldn't see them anywhere.

Suddenly she panicked: all she wanted to do was escape. She couldn't stand it if after everything the men woke up, saw what had happened and made them captives again. 'Hurry!' Pulling Lizzie after her she tiptoed as quickly as possible out of the camp, into the trees. At once they were surrounded by darkness. No shout came from behind them and she almost fainted with relief.

Lizzie stopped her. 'But, miss, we're out in the middle of nowhere. We're lost. Without a horse we'll never get any place.'

'It's a chance we must take. I'm not going back there.'

Lizzie didn't want to do so either. 'Which way?'

'Have you any idea where we are?'

'No.' Lizzie shook her head, staring into the black night that enveloped them. 'But we didn't come very far into the trees before those bastards made camp. If we go back the same way we'll soon find ourselves in the desert. We'll be easy to spot there. We should head further into the trees.'

'Yes. Let's put as much distance as possible between us and Hennessey.'

It sounded easy but the going was harder than either girl imagined. Bushes and brambles were in their way, catching at their clothes, scratching their arms and legs. Roots of trees threatened to trip them up. They had to push their way through dense undergrowth. And they were soon exhausted, filthy and thirsty.

'This is hopeless,' Thora said, with a little sob. 'We're hardly making any progress at all.'

'I think we're still quite near the camp,' Lizzie agreed. 'Oh, miss, I can hardly go another step.'

'Nor me. Shall we find a place to hide where we won't be found?' Thora didn't consider that a very good idea but her tired brain refused to come up with anything better. And what was the alternative?

16

'Where are they? Where are the damn bitches gone?'

As soon as Old Man Hennessey woke up and saw Thora and Lizzie were no longer his prisoners he lost his temper, utterly and completely. Face red with fury he shouted, 'Damn you both, you've let 'em get away.'

He started kicking out at anything that came within reach: mugs and plates, saddles, the remains of the camp-fire. He would have kicked Frank and Jack too if he could have got to them.

'Hell, you damn idiots can't do nothing right. They've escaped and I hadn't finished with 'em. Hell, I hadn't hardly started!'

Swearing he stomped around the small clearing while wisely Frank and Jack kept well out of his way.

'Which of you idiots was meant to tie 'em up?' At last Hennessey came to a halt and stood, hands on his hips, glaring at the O'Connors.

In an effort to protect Jack, because who knew what Hennessey was capable of, Frank said, 'It don't matter now. They've gone, is all.'

That wasn't what Hennessey wanted to hear. 'How the hell did I ever get involved with you? Two fools who can't even tie up a couple of girls properly! I'm ashamed to think you're kin of mine!'

'OK, let it rest.' Frank was close to losing his own temper. 'If you were so worried about 'em you should've tied 'em up yourself.'

That was also the wrong thing to say and Hennessey's eyes narrowed until they were little more than slits in his face.

Before he could start shouting again Frank went on, 'Never mind about 'em now. They've escaped and there ain't nothing we can do 'bout it.'

Hennessey glared even harder. 'What the hell d'you mean?' He pointed at the brothers. 'I ain't leaving here till I've found 'em.'

'We ain't got time for that,' Frank protested.

'Time, time,' Hennessey mimicked. 'What is it with you and time?'

'It's true, we must get on.' Or they would be too late to commit the perfect robbery.

'Hell, Frank, it ain't as if they can've gone far. Anyway.' A crafty look crossed Hennessey's face, the scar standing out white and ugly. 'You don't want 'em telling all and sundry 'bout your damn plan to rob the silver mine in Cotton Creek, do you?'

'That ain't the plan — ' Jack began.

'Who can they tell?' Frank interrupted. 'Like you say there ain't no one coming after us no more. And they're two girls alone, on foot.' He glanced at the horses to make sure all three were still there. 'They don't know where they are or where they can go to for help.

Hell, Bernie, there ain't anywhere within walking distance they can go.'

'So?'

'So quite likely they'll get completely lost and die out in the desert.' Frank wasn't certain he liked that thought but at the same time the girls really weren't his problem; he hadn't wanted them along. 'But if by chance they do manage to reach someone who'll help 'em it'll've taken 'em so long that by then it'll be too late for anyone to stop us and we'll've carried out our plan and be well away. You'll even be enjoying yourself in Mexico. C'mon, Bernie. OK, so they've escaped but this job is more important. Think of the money.'

Hennessey didn't reply. However much money was involved nothing could be more important than him getting his own back on those who had done him and his family down. And, while they might not realize it, the O'Connor brothers were rapidly in danger of joining that list.

'OK, Bernie?'

'Yeah, I guess.' He spoke sullenly.

Frank and Jack glanced at one another in relief. 'But while you pack up I'll go and look for 'em.' He wasn't giving in that easily.

'But . . . '

'I won't be long.' The man grinned. 'And iffen I find 'em then we'll all have what we want, won't we?'

'God,' Jack said, once Hennessey had disappeared amongst the trees. 'I feared we was dead then.' He wiped his face free of sweat.

'Me too. Mebbe, Jack, it'd've been better if you'd tied up those girls so they couldn't get away.'

Jack reddened with embarrassment that he had been got the better of by two young women.

'You didn't let 'em get away on purpose, did you?'

'Hell, no! I can't understand it. I thought . . . '

'Never mind. I can't say I'm sorry they ain't in Hennessey's clutches any longer. And having 'em along was slowing us down. Let's pack. Get goin' before the Old Man changes his mind.'

Jack nodded eagerly. The sooner this was all over the better as far as he was concerned.

★ ★ ★

Still in a fine temper Hennessey stalked away from the camp. It had taken all his control not to draw his gun and shoot the two brothers. The only reason he didn't was because he wanted to get his hands on the silver they kept promising him, and they'd best be talking true.

The trail Thora and Lizzie had left behind them was clear to see, because in their haste and in the dark they'd broken twigs and trampled ferns. There was even a footprint here and there. He grinned. This was going to be easier than he'd thought. He'd catch them and when he did . . .

'Miss Dowling!' he called. 'Lizzie. Where the hell are you? I'm coming after you. Show yourselves and I'll go easy on you. Iffen you keep on hiding you can't even imagine how hard I'll make it. I ain't far away. I'll find you. Come on out, girlies.'

A little way up ahead Thora and Lizzie crouched amongst a thick clump of prickly bushes, clutching one another in fear, clearly able to hear the man as he made his noisy way towards them. Thora was dismayed because they hadn't gone nearly as far as she'd thought and hoped; in fact they were still quite near the camp. They had been able to hear Hennessey shouting at Frank and Jack, even though they hadn't been able to make out the words, expect there seemed to be a lot of swearing. Now Hennessey was getting closer with every step.

'Should we move?' Lizzie whispered.

'No. He'll hear us if we do.'

Tears began to slip down Lizzie's cheeks and Thora held her close, feeling her shaking. Suddenly Hennessey's shadow loomed across them, he only had to look to his right and he would spot them. Thora bit down on a gasp of fright and put a hand over Lizzie's mouth to prevent her making a sound.

The man came to a halt so his legs were inches from Thora's face.

'Bernie!' It was Frank. 'We're ready to leave.'

'Just a few more minutes.'

'No, now! We won't wait for you and we're taking all three horses.'

Hennessey swore long and loudly. He looked as if he didn't know what to do — to stay to look for Thora and Lizzie, or leave. In the end he decided Frank would carry out his threat and, not wanting to be left out here by himself, he made up his mind to go with the O'Connors.

'I'll get the two of you yet!' he yelled. Swearing some more he turned on his heel and stamped back the way he had come.

Neither Thora nor Lizzie hardly dared breathe until he had disappeared amongst the trees.

It wasn't long before they heard the

three men ride away. Thora slumped to the ground, trembling all over, while Lizzie wiped her eyes, then started crying again.

After a little while the girl raised her tear-stained face and said, 'Miss Dowling, have they really gone? Or is it a trap?'

'I think they must have left. I haven't heard anything for a while, have you?' Lizzie shook her head. 'And I doubt they could keep that quiet. They'd make some noise. And Frank was so eager to be on his way I can't see him waiting around to find out if we put in an appearance. Besides, why should they try and trick us?' Thora convinced herself. 'No, they must have gone. Shall we go and find out? But let's be quiet just in case they are still there.'

Thora feared her legs were shaking so much they wouldn't support her but somehow she got to her feet and helped Lizzie up beside her. As quietly and carefully as they could they made their way back to the camp.

It was empty.

'Hooray!' Lizzie cried joyfully.

Thora said nothing, she knew their troubles weren't yet over. In fact in some ways they'd just started. They had no horses, nothing to eat or drink. Didn't know where they were.

Lizzie left her side to search the camp. 'They haven't left anything behind we can use,' she said in disgust. 'What shall we do?'

'Well, we can't stay here. Our best bet is to go back to the trail we were following yesterday. If a posse is on its way that's where it'll be, isn't it?'

'Yeah, Miss Dowling.'

'And it was open country that way too. We'll make better progress there. We won't get far if we try to find a way through all these trees and bushes.'

Thora tried to sound sure of herself, knew she had to pretend she was hopeful of rescue for the sake of the other girl. But she wasn't hopeful at all.

17

No one could remember which came
first: the town of Cotton Creek or the
silver mine. Now one served the other.
The mine provided employment for a
large number of men and the town
provided goods and enjoyment for the
miners.

Hennessey and the O'Connor brothers arrived there in the middle of the
afternoon.

Cotton Creek could hardly be called
a town. It was more a speck in the
middle of a group of low dusty hills
which were dotted here and there with
cotton-wood trees, cactus and sagebrush.
Its one street meandered between the
town's buildings. At one end was a livery
stable and at the other a general store,
while in between were two saloons, a
tiny brothel and an even tinier hotel.
They were interspersed with a few houses

of various sizes and some tents. At this time of day the street was more or less empty, with just a couple of men hanging about outside one of the saloons while everyone else kept indoors out of the sun.

In Hennessey's view the best thing, in fact the only good thing, about the place was that he saw no sign of any law. Otherwise he wondered what on earth he was doing here, especially with no sign of the silver mine they'd come to rob either.

'It's out of town,' Frank said, as they rode down to the stable. ''Bout a mile or two away. Look, Bernie, let's leave the horses and go and get us a beer. Then we can talk 'bout what we're goin' to do.'

'We staying here tonight?' Hennessey dismounted.

'Yeah, why?' Jack asked.

'Wondered where we was goin' to stay.' He doubted they'd be welcomed at the hotel, rough and ready though it was.

'We usually sleep in rooms at the back of the saloon. Or mebbe at the brothel.' Frank grinned. 'The girls there ain't that young or that pretty, but they're cheap.'

Hennessey smirked back. That sounded more like it. They stabled the horses and, as they strolled back to the saloons, he said, 'So when we goin' to rob the mine?'

Frank shrugged and grinned at Jack. 'Who said we was goin' to rob the mine?'

Hennessey came to a halt. His good mood was instantly replaced by bad and his hands clenched into fists. 'Then what the hell are we doin' in this godforsaken place? I hope you ain't brought me here on a damn wild goose chase.'

'Don't worry,' Frank said quickly before Hennessey could lose his temper. 'We're robbing the mine — '

'You just damn well said we weren't!'

' — but not of silver.'

Hennessey sighed heavily. He wished

he could shoot Frank for being so mysterious and Jack for sniggering. He felt they were laughing at him and he didn't like that. 'Talk plain,' he snarled. 'Or don't bother.'

'It's OK,' Jack said. 'You'll soon find out what we mean. And then you'll want to go along with us right enough.'

'I hope so. For your damn sakes.'

★ ★ ★

Archie Wymark finished his mug of coffee, throwing the dregs on the fire. He looked round at the other three men. 'Should be back in Cotton Creek by tomorrow afternoon.'

The men glanced at one another and smiled. On each of these journeys Wymark almost always said the same thing after they'd almost always stopped at this same place.

'So let's get going.' He got to his feet and went over to his horse, patting its neck. 'The miners are waiting for their money so they can pay off their debts.'

He nearly always said that as well.

More snickers.

'Ready?' Wymark took no notice of them. 'Keep your eyes open,' he warned.

They would soon be entering the hills around Cotton Creek, which he considered to be the most dangerous part of the journey. Not only were there plenty of places outlaws could wait in ambush but they were near enough to home to start becoming careless. He eased the rifle in its scabbard, making sure he could pull it out without it catching on anything. Then he kicked his horse forward and led the small group of men out onto the trail. He was aware they were sure he worried over nothing, that as they'd never yet experienced any trouble it was unlikely they ever would, but he wasn't about to take any chances.

* * *

'So what the hell is this damn plan of yours all about?' Hennessey downed his beer in one swallow and leant back in his seat surveying the room.

The saloon wasn't up to much. It was small and cramped and like the rest of Cotton Creek it was boring. Apart from him and the O'Connors there were just a few men — miners by their clothes — over by the bar, laughing and talking to a middle-aged woman. Hennessey hoped the whores in the brothel were better looking and younger than she was! But at least the beer was cold and it made a change to sit at a table and be able to drink in peace without being scared a marshal would come in and want to arrest him.

Frank leant forward so no one would hear him. 'The silver mine employs quite a lot of miners. At least thirty. Probably more. Ain't that right, Jack?'

'Yeah, we tried to get work there but — '

'Get on with it!' Hennessey thumped the table.

'It'd be too risky to rob the mine of silver. They employ guards to patrol all round it and they look real mean. Anyway, how would we sell it? Who to? But, Bernie, the men have to be paid, don't they?'

'They wouldn't work there for nothing,' Jack put in.

Hennessey grimaced but managed to say nothing about stupid remarks.

'So 'bout once every three months, Wymark, the assistant manager, leads some men into Tucson to collect the payroll.'

'How many men?' Hennessey perked up.

'Three, four at most. A guard and a couple of ordinary miners. There's at least two thousand dollars involved and we've heard that mostly it's double that, perhaps even as much as five thousand dollars because the payroll also includes money to pay for equipment and supplies, that sorta thing. Think about it, Bernie, five thousand dollars!'

Hennessey's eyes opened a little wider. Not the fortune he'd been expecting from the way the brothers had boasted how the amount would change their lives. Obviously they had different ideas to him about how much money would be needed for that. But it was enough, more than enough. He could ride down into Mexico and impress the *señoritas*, find shelter some place nice and cosy till his escape from the law was forgotten. It might be a risky job, that was obviously why these two idiots had helped him escape because they daren't do it alone, but it was worth taking the risk.

'So?' he said pretending he didn't understand.

'So,' Frank said, 'that's what we're goin' to rob: the payroll.'

He and Jack grinned. Hennessey thought it was obvious they both believed he was stupid. Well, so had a lot of others and they'd always paid the price.

18

Thora didn't know what she and Lizzie were going to do. Eventually they had found their way out of the trees and into the open, where they stopped, flopping down on the ground, to get their breath back and rest for a while. Their faces and arms were scratched from the brambles, the hems of their skirts torn.

'There's no sign of Hennessey and the two brothers,' Lizzie said, sighing in relief.

But, Thora thought, neither was there a sign of anyone or anything else. No posse. Not even the Wells Fargo stagecoach. No help.

'Which way shall we go?' Lizzie asked, after a few moments.

'Back towards Freeman's stage station,' Thora decided. 'Away from the direction Hennessey was going in.

That's that way isn't it?' She pointed eastwards.

'Yeah. OK, miss, let's go.' Lizzie sounded much more cheerful, more like her old self, now she was free of Hennessey and his threats.

But Thora could find nothing cheerful in their situation. Although she didn't say so to Lizzie, in her heart she knew they didn't stand a chance of making it to Freeman's. It had taken a whole day to ride to this spot from the stage station, it would take them days to walk back. Without food or water. And it was so hot with no shade or relief from the sun that beat mercilessly down on them. She could barely breathe. Perhaps they should have stayed amongst the trees after all, at least it had been cooler there. But what was the point of that?

They started walking. They walked for most of the morning; their walking had become nothing but a stagger and they were making little or no headway, when Thora suddenly gave up. She sank to the ground.

'Miss Dowling!'

'Oh, Lizzie, I simply can't go any further. It's no use.' She put her head in her hands, a picture of dejection. 'We'll never get there.'

She had done her best to keep hopeful for Lizzie's sake but it was difficult when she was exhausted, hungry and, worst of all, so thirsty her mouth was parched dry and her tongue swollen. Both shoes had holes in the bottoms and her feet were badly blistered. Her skin was burnt from the sun and every bone in her body ached.

Lizzie sank down beside her and started to cry.

It wasn't fair. They had escaped Hennessey's clutches and now they were going to die in the middle of nowhere with no one to ever know . . .

★　★　★

'There's still no sign of them,' Kirkpatrick complained. 'I'd hoped we would have spotted something of them

155

before now. Where are they? I hope we haven't lost them.'

'They were some way in front of us,' Pitt pointed out. 'And they know where they're going, we're having to follow their tracks.'

'But it's the middle of the afternoon already. If we're not lucky soon we'll have to camp out for another night without knowing what's happening to the girls.' Kirkpatrick wasn't sure he could stand that.

'I know . . . wait!' Pitt pulled his horse to a halt and leaning over the saddlehorn peered forward.

Kirkpatrick's stomach twisted painfully. 'What is it?'

'I spotted something or someone. I think.'

'Who is it? How many?'

'I don't know. I might be wrong.'

They rode forward a little way, their eyes searching the horizon, before coming to another stop.

'No, there.' Pitt glanced at Kirkpatrick. 'It looks a lot like a couple of people.'

Kirkpatrick still couldn't make out anything through the heat-haze. 'Can you see who it is?' He found his heart was thumping with fear or hope, he wasn't sure which.

'No, they're too far away.'

'Are they alive?' Please, Kirkpatrick thought, don't let Elias have seen two bodies. He glanced up at the sky. There was no sign of vultures circulating above.

'I'm sorry, Ralph, I can't tell.'

Kirkpatrick's heart skipped a beat. Who would be out here on foot except Thora and Lizzie; or maybe Apaches?

Pitt turned a puzzled face towards him. 'It can't be the girls, can it? How would they have gotten away from Hennessey? He wouldn't just let them go, would he?'

'Let's find out,' Kirkpatrick said, needing desperately to discover whether it was Thora and Lizzie. 'But be careful,' he added, in case it was Apaches.

They dug spurs into the horses' sides.

'Miss Dowling, look!'

'No, I don't care.'

'Miss, please.' Lizzie clutched at Thora's arm, dragging her up, supporting her. 'Two riders. There in the distance.'

'I can't see anything,' Thora said sulkily. 'You're imagining things.'

'No, I'm not.'

'It's not Hennessey, is it?' Sudden fear stabbed at Thora.

'No. They're coming from the opposite way. And there's only two of 'em. It's help, whoever it is.'

'Are they coming in this direction? We'd better attract their attention.' Thora didn't think she could bear it if help was so close at hand and then passed them by. She started waving her arms.

★ ★ ★

'It is them!' Pitt shouted in relief.

'Are they hurt?' But Kirkpatrick

could see for himself that they weren't. 'Thora!' he yelled, and kicked his horse into a faster gallop.

★ ★ ★

'It's OK, miss. They've seen us. Oh, miss!' Lizzie suddenly shrieked. 'Oh, it's Elias!' She hugged Thora. 'Elias, here!' She jumped up and down.

Thora hardly dared allow herself to hope that the other rider was Ralph, for fear she would be disappointed. It had to be one of the townsmen, didn't it? But surely Mr Pitt couldn't have taken Ralph's body back to Felicidad and then ridden all this way in such a short time? And if he had, wouldn't more than one townsman have accompanied him?

Oh, please let Hennessey have been wrong and please let it be Ralph.

And then all at once she could see for herself that the other rider was Ralph, unhurt, riding to her rescue just as she had always known he would. Her legs were unable to support her any longer and she sank to the ground again. She began to cry, tears of relief and happiness.

19

It was a matter of moments before the two men reached Thora and Lizzie. Kirkpatrick was throwing himself off his horse and racing towards Thora even while she was struggling to her feet and running towards him.

'Ralph, oh Ralph, thank God you're still alive,' she sobbed. As his arms enclosed around her she thought she never wanted him to let her go again.

Pitt hurried over to Lizzie who collapsed against him. 'Hush, hush,' he comforted her. He looked at the bruises on her face and wished that Hennessey was present so he could give him some of his own medicine. He saw her dry and cracked lips and quickly took hold of his canteen of water and passed it to her. 'Just a sip.'

'Thora, sweetheart, are you all right?' Kirkpatrick asked at last, thinking that at least she wasn't blaming him for her ordeal. He held her at arm's length, staring at her anxiously. 'They didn't hurt you?'

Thora knew he was asking if she had been raped. Shuddering at the thought, she said, 'No one touched me.' She hoped Ralph believed her, especially as, thank God, it was the truth. 'Honestly.'

Kirkpatrick nodded; he could tell that for himself from the way Thora was behaving, the way she looked. He hugged her close in relief.

'I can't say the same for poor Lizzie. Hennessey ill-treated her, although thankfully the other two left her alone. Actually they took hardly any notice of us but they were dirty and smelt so bad . . . Oh, Ralph, I was so scared and then I thought you were dead. Hennessey said he'd shot you.' Thora started crying again. 'I didn't know what I'd do without you.'

'It's all right,' Kirkpatrick said, stroking her hair. 'It's over now. You're safe and I'm not hurt.'

'But you are.' Thora noticed the dried blood on his shirt. 'You have been shot.'

'No, Hennessey missed me but my horse was spooked and I fell off and the old wound opened up. It's stopped bleeding now.' In the joy of finding Thora he'd forgotten completely all about his painful shoulder.

'Did you find the pieces of my handkerchief?'

'I've got them here.' Kirkpatrick patted his jacket pocket. 'Without them we would've headed for Mexico.'

'It was all I could think of to do.'

'It was very helpful. And so clever.'

His arm around Lizzie supporting her, Pitt came over. 'Let's get these girls something to eat and drink — '

'Oh, yes,' Thora said. 'We're parched. We haven't had anything to drink since yesterday evening.' With relief she took the canteen from Lizzie.

' — and then we can decide what to do.'

'There's some trees just up ahead,' Lizzie said. 'It'll be cooler if we shelter under them. I can't stand this heat.'

'A good idea,' Kirkpatrick said. He wanted to do all he could to make both girls comfortable after their ordeal. He led Thora over to his horse. 'Then you can tell us how you escaped. Are you OK to ride, sweetheart?'

'Oh yes.' Now she was safe with Ralph, knew he was unhurt, Thora felt better. Felt alive again.

'Come on, Lizzie, you can ride with me.' Pitt brought up the two horses and helped the girl into the saddle.

Before long the four of them were sitting around a fire eating some of the rations Kirkpatrick had brought with him and drinking coffee. Afterwards they swopped stories.

Kirkpatrick was awfully proud of Thora. Despite how terrified she must have been she had kept her head, taken charge and looked after Lizzie. Had managed to get them away from Hennessey. Although what would have happened if he and Pitt hadn't come along when they did . . . He closed his mind on that thought.

'Oh, Ralph,' Thora said. 'I can't believe that poor Dave Vaughan is dead. I prayed that Hennessey was lying about that.'

'I'm afraid it's true.'

'What about Mrs Barron?'

'It didn't look like she was badly hurt. She was conscious when we were at the boarding-house.'

'Thank God. Was anyone else shot or hurt in the explosion?'

'Luckily no.' Catching hold of Thora's hand, Kirkpatrick went on, 'Have you any idea where Hennessey was going? Why he didn't head for Mexico?'

'And who the two men were who rescued Hennessey?' Pitt added.

Thora rested her head on Kirkpatrick's shoulder. 'The two men were called Frank and Jack. They were some sort of relatives of Hennessey.'

'I heard Bernie speak about them before,' Lizzie said. 'Their surname is O'Connor and they're his distant cousins. Originally they came from

Texas. Then they did something bad there and were wanted by the law, so they moved into Arizona. Bernie was annoyed because they'd helped him with rustling cattle over near El Paso.'

'They might have rescued Hennessey but none of them was getting on any too well,' Thora said. 'In fact, they seemed to regret what they'd done.'

'And Bernie seemed to regret being rescued by them!' Lizzie said, and added hopefully, 'Perhaps they'll all shoot one another.'

'I can't say I've ever heard of the O'Connors,' Kirkpatrick said. 'But I daresay there might be a Wanted poster for them back at the office. What about where they were going? Do you know?'

'Yes. To a place called Cotton Creek. It sounded like it was near Nogales.'

Lizzie nodded.

'I know where it is,' Pitt spoke up. 'I passed through it a couple of years ago on my way to somewhere else.' He made it sound as if it was always a place to be passed through and never stopped at. 'I should've remembered, Ralph, when we were talking about silver mines in the area, there's one near Cotton Creek.'

'That's right, Mr Pitt, and they're going to rob it. At least that's what it sounded like.' Thora paused. 'Ralph, we are going back to Felicidad, aren't we?' There was a little tremor in her voice.

'Oh, sweetheart, I don't see how I can.'

Although she wasn't surprised by his reply, Thora's heart sank.

'Hennessey and his friends are planning a robbery. The three of them have shown themselves willing to kill to get what they want and innocent people might be hurt. I wouldn't be much of a lawman if I didn't do my best to prevent them carrying it out. Or if I'm too late to do that, at least help to catch them afterwards, especially if Cotton Creek is too small to have much in the way of law.'

'Couldn't you telegraph them?'

'First we don't know whether a line

goes into Cotton Creek and secondly by the time we got back to Felicidad to send a message the robbery would be over and Hennessey long gone. And I *must* do my best to catch him before he disappears into Mexico. I'd feel I'd let down everyone in Felicidad if I didn't. Thora, dear, all the while he's alive he'll pose a threat to us. And to Felicidad. He must be brought to justice. What do you think, Elias? What do you want to do?'

'I guess I could take the girls back but I'd sooner stick with you and see this through.' In Pitt's mind Hennessey had to be punished for all he'd done and he wanted to be there to see it happen.

Thora didn't know whether to be pleased or sorry. She wasn't going home just yet but at least Ralph wouldn't be out here chasing Hennessey and the O'Connors and risking his life on his own. More importantly, she didn't want to go back to Felicidad without him.

'Besides,' Pitt went on, 'Cotton Creek is closer than Felicidad and Miss Dowling and Lizzie need to rest for a while.'

And tidy up, Thora thought, staring down at her broken shoes, dusty skirt and torn blouse. And have a bath! She'd never felt so filthy. And wash and comb her hair. Ease away the tensions of the last few days.

'I don't want to go anywhere where Bernie is.' Lizzie spoke quietly.

Pitt squeezed her arm. 'By the time we get to Cotton Creek I don't reckon he'll still be there. It ain't his sort of place and he won't want to hang around, especially if he's just committed a robbery. You don't want him to get away do you? Like Ralph says, while he's at large none of us will be free of his threat.'

'I know, but . . . '

'Look, if you really want me to I will take you both back to Felicidad.'

'No, Mr Pitt,' Thora interrupted quickly. 'You two must stick together.

It's the only way. Lizzie, dear, Ralph and Mr Pitt won't let Hennessey get near us.'

'We certainly won't,' Pitt said.

'OK,' Lizzie agreed, although she sounded unhappy.

Thora took a deep breath. 'Ralph, you mustn't worry about us. Your job is to catch Hennessey.'

Kirkpatrick kissed her lightly on the cheek, knowing she was doing her best to hide her own fears. 'Elias, you say you know where Cotton Creek is?'

'Yeah, I think I remember the way. It ain't too far.'

'Good. We'll rest up here for the night and set out in the morning.'

20

'This is where Jack and me thought we'd hit 'em.' Frank indicated the brow of a hill.

The trail leading up from the valley to this point was quite steep, which meant any riders would be coming slowly and would probably be spread out.

'We can wait on this side, hidden by those rocks over there, and be out of the miners' sight till they get close. They won't be expecting to be dry-gulched, especially this near to the mine. They'll be thinking of getting back to spend their money. All that'll make 'em an easy target. We'll have 'em in our sights before they know anything's wrong.'

Frank realized he was gabbling but that was only because Old Man Hennessey was glaring round, ready to find fault with the place, the ambush and the whole scheme.

It was early morning and chilly still. Hennessey hadn't liked being rousted from the bed of the whore at the brothel. He never liked getting up early anyway, and he certainly hadn't wanted to ride all this way before eating breakfast and drinking several cups of coffee. He preferred getting his money the easiest way possible by letting others do the hard work, while he sat back and enjoyed himself.

'You sure this is the way they'll come?' he growled. Actually he thought it was a good spot for an ambush but he wasn't about to let the brothers know that.

'Yeah. After we done learnt about the payroll we made sure we was in this area the last two times when they went to collect it so we could watch 'em. On both occasions they came this way and more or less at the same hour of the day too.'

'Only I wouldn't like to be out here

wasting my time.' Hennessey hoped the brothers were right and thought they probably were. This was the quickest way back to the mine.

'You won't be.'

'C'mon, Bernie, trust us,' Jack added. 'There mightn't be any sign of 'em yet but that's because we're here in good time to lay our ambush. They'll be coming along soon enough. So let's get these horses outa sight and lie in wait.'

'And, Bernie, make sure not to do anything until the riders get near the top of the hill. We don't want nothing to go wrong.'

'Yeah, sure,' Hennessey agreed with a frown.

★   ★   ★

Wymark stared up at the hill in front of them. It was now light, yet parts of the valley still lay in deep shadow. He wished there was another route they could take but to skirt the hill would add at least half a day to the journey.

And by now the men with him were always so anxious to get home they wouldn't appreciate being made to ride further than they had to. Once beyond the ridge he always breathed a sigh of relief, knowing that the rest of the ride to the mine where they could see for miles around was unlikely to pose any danger.

'Keep up, keep together,' he urged the men. The guard went to the front while he brought up the rear so he could make sure there were no stragglers. 'Careful.' He wondered if they really listened to him.

* * *

'Here they come,' Frank said, note of excitement in his voice. 'Steady. Shoot to kill.'

'I know damn well what to do,' Hennessey said angrily. He shifted slightly and his elbow dislodged a stone, sending it skittering down the hill.

'You fool!'

Alerted, Wymark looked up. He saw movement ahead of them. 'Watch out!' he yelled. 'Dismount.'

At the same time a rifle barked. The guard flung up his arms and fell backwards off his horse, landing heavily.

Dragging his rifle from its scabbard, Wymark slid out of the saddle and threw himself down, hugging the ground. The other two miners did the same and were already firing back at their attackers. But while there wasn't a great deal of shelter on the hillside the outlaws above them were hidden behind rocks and trees and didn't present much of a target.

'Save your ammo! Make sure of your shots!'

★ ★ ★

'Get on down there.' Frank nudged Hennessey in the side.

'Me? Why the hell me?'

'Because you alerted 'em. Go on.' Normally Frank wouldn't have dared speak to Hennessey like that, but he was angry in case his carelessness had cost them the chance to seize the payroll.

Swearing under his breath and crouching low, Hennessey moved out of his hiding place and around the rocks until he had a better view of the two miners highest up the hill. He raised his rifle, aimed and fired. The bullet hit the nearest man in the arm. The man jerked upright and from above both Frank and Jack fired at him. He went down under several bullets.

Scared, in a panic, his companion leapt to his feet.

'Stay where you are!' Wymark called to him.

The young man took no notice. Wide-eyed with fear he turned to run and was shot in the back. He fell and lay still in a heap. There were shouts of triumph from the ambushers.

Wymark was in his own panic. He

was alone and while he sent several shots towards the outlaws he knew he couldn't beat them by himself. What should he do? If he stayed he would be shot for sure, but if he ran he might live to report the attack. Either way the payroll would be stolen, although right then that was the least of his worries. Followed by several bullets kicking up spouts of earth all round him he inched down the hill a little way.

He glanced round, wondering if he could reach his horse, and saw with sinking heart that he couldn't. All four horses had galloped off and, while they had now come to a halt, they were a long way off. Perhaps if he ran towards the animals the outlaws would consider him as no longer a threat and be satisfied with the money and let him go. It was his only chance. He got slowly to his feet, laying his rifle down on the ground.

Probably the O'Connors wouldn't have bothered about him. They had the payroll and while the thought of killing didn't trouble them they mostly only did it when it was necessary. Hennessey was another matter. His bloodlust was roused. He wanted to kill and keep on killing. Standing, he raised his rifle. Fired.

The bullet struck Wymark in the leg. He cried out with sudden shock and searing pain, and, his leg collapsing beneath him, he tripped, falling forward. His arms reached out but grabbed only at empty air. With a scream of fear he found himself tumbling to the bottom of the hill. It wasn't very far, but his fall seemed to go on forever as he bashed against rocks and hard earth. He came to a stop with an awkward thump and blacked out for a moment.

★ ★ ★

Hennessey punched the air. Frank and Jack exchanged glances of satisfaction. Their plan had succeeded. It was certainly handy to have a killing machine like Hennessey along, even if he'd nearly fouled things up.

As Frank joined him, Hennessey said sarcastically, 'You'd best get their horses.'

'Why?' Jack asked, and immediately wished he hadn't as Hennessey turned to scowl at him.

'Because, you damn idiot, the money we've come all this way to steal will be in the saddle-bags on the horses. That's why. Or did you think it'd be carried in the men's pockets? Bloody fools.'

Frank wanted to tell Hennessey that having to shoot the men before they came near enough to grab the horses before they could run off was his fault. But it was one thing to criticize him in the heat of battle and quite another to do so afterwards and he didn't dare.

★　★　★

From where he lay, Wymark turned his head slightly and watched his attackers making their way down the hill towards him. He was in agony, the bullet had struck him in the thigh and there seemed to be an awful lot of blood soaking his trouser leg, and he was very scared. These men were ruthless, wouldn't hesitate to finish him off. He thought that in the fall he must have broken his arm, it certainly hurt, almost worse than his leg. He couldn't even stand, let alone run anywhere. Even if he crawled over to the boulders lying at the bottom of the hill and there found a place to conceal himself, what would be the use of that? All the ambushers need do was follow the trail of blood he'd leave behind.

They were almost on him!

Wymark could think of doing only one thing. He curled up and pretended to be dead already.

While Jack led their horses down the hill, Hennessey and Frank followed behind arguing about what to do next. All three were eager to find out how much money they'd stolen and they passed Wymark by with barely a second glance.

At first Wymark could hardly believe his good fortune and he watched with thumping heart, sure they would turn back, as the outlaws rode to where the other animals had stopped. He was safe.

Well, not safe exactly. He was stuck out in the open, shot in the leg and with a broken arm, and no way to get back to Cotton Creek.

But at least he was alive, which was more than could be said for his three companions. He rested his head on the dusty earth and closed his eyes.

★ ★ ★

Once they reached the miners' horses, the O'Connors dismounted and caught up the reins. Their eyes lit up. Four of the saddle-bags were bulging!

'We done it!' Jack said, capering around. 'We done robbed the silver mine!'

'Hurry it up,' Hennessey said. 'Divide the saddle-bags between us and let's be on our way.'

Frank was surprised. 'Don't you want to count the money? See how much we stole?'

''Course I do. But the first thing is to get away from here in case some of the miners come to find out what's happened to their payroll.'

'They won't miss it yet,' Frank objected.

'Do you wanna take the chance? Anyhow, you clowns are likely to take so long counting the money that they'll arrive afore you finish. There you'll be gloating over it and getting shot at the same time. 'Sides I want my breakfast and we can't wait here to boil up coffee. We need somewhere a bit more sheltered. Bring the miners' horses. We can sell 'em once we get to Mexico and so make even more money.'

Frank wasn't pleased at Hennessey telling them what to do, or making out that they didn't know their trade of robbing and killing.

'Never mind,' Jack whispered to him. 'We'll soon be free of him.'

Frank nodded. He had absolutely no intention of accompanying Old Man Hennessey to Mexico, or anywhere else for that matter.

21

It had taken longer than either Pitt or Kirkpatrick hoped it would to reach Cotton Creek.

First off, although they'd started out as soon as dawn lit the sky, they hadn't liked to rush Thora and Lizzie after all they'd been through, for both girls were exhausted. Then Pitt, who wasn't that sure of the direction in which the town lay, missed the turn-off, with the result that they had to backtrack for quite a distance.

Kirkpatrick fretted the whole morning, scared Hennessey would make good his escape and not be easily found; maybe not found at all. But all at once just after noon they reached the creek, after which it was a simple matter to follow the road, and they arrived in the town after another hour's travel.

Where everything looked quiet.

'Nothing's happened here,' Pitt said, as they rode up the street towards the hotel. His hand hovered near his gun but now he relaxed.

'What are you going to do?' Thora asked. She was so tired she was almost asleep in the saddle, leaning her head against Kirkpatrick's chest.

He glanced at Pitt. The two men wanted to visit the silver mine, go after Hennessey, but Thora and Lizzie were their first concern.

'Let's get you two girls a room at the hotel, so you can wash and rest.'

'And we need something to wear. We can't go around like this.' Thora indicated the clothes she and Lizzie were wearing. 'They're like filthy rags.' She hoped Ralph wouldn't think she was complaining about her appearance when he had so much more of importance on his mind, but she really couldn't bear to wear what she had on a moment longer than was necessary.

'I expect the general store we passed

back there will have some clothes for sale.'

'But how will you pay?'

'Don't you worry about that.' Pitt grinned. 'When Ralph and me ran out of The Silver Dollar to see what the explosion was about I'd just won several poker games and luckily I'd picked up all my winnings.' He jingled his pocket. 'I've still got the money with me.'

Thora smiled in relief.

'Elias,' Lizzie said nervously, glancing round, 'Hennessey and the other two ain't here, are they?'

Pitt squeezed her arm. 'No, sweetheart, they'll want to rob the mine and be off.'

'But it don't look like they have robbed it yet,' Lizzie pointed out. 'There would be some disturbance on the street if they had, not just everyone going about their normal business. I'm frightened. I don't want to meet up with Bernie again.'

'Nor do I,' Thora added, with a

shiver. 'And Lizzie's right.'

'Neither of you will come to any harm, I promise,' Kirkpatrick said. 'Hennessey won't be at the hotel even if he is in town. And like Elias I'm sure he's not here.' Which he thought was a pity. He wanted to deal with the Old Man once and for all.

And with that both girls had to be satisfied.

But Kirkpatrick was right. When they went into the hotel and he asked the clerk if he had seen three strangers in the last couple of days, the clerk immediately shook his head.

'If any strangers have arrived in Cotton Creek they ain't come in here.'

'There, it's all right,' Pitt said to Lizzie, who smiled uncertainly.

'Have you two rooms we can have?' Kirkpatrick went on.

'Sure do.'

Thora added, 'Do you have a bathroom?'

'Not a bathroom, no, but my wife'll let you use the tin bath in the kitchen. Is that OK?'

'Oh, yes, please.' Thora couldn't wait to get clean.

'You folks look like you've had some trouble,' the clerk said, as he led the way up the steep staircase to the two rooms he'd given them — the only rooms the hotel had.

'Yes, with the three men I mentioned. I'm marshal over at Felicidad and two of them broke my prisoner out of jail.'

'Not Bernie Hennessey?' The clerk's eyes widened.

'That's right. You've heard about him here?'

'Oh, yeah, only too well. He's a troublemaker, him and his family both. His kids were killed a while ago, weren't they? Were you the ones did that?'

'Yeah, me and Elias here.'

'Then God bless you both.' The clerk shook their hands, before a worried look appeared on his face. 'And now you think he's on his way here? What for?'

'Probably to rob your silver mine.'

'Oh God!'

'Do you have any law here?'

'No, I suppose the nearest thing we've got to the law, at least here in town although they do employ guards out at the mine, is Mr Temple, who owns the general store. At least he's the one we usually turn to 'bout town affairs.'

'We've got to visit him anyway so we'll warn him to keep his eyes open. Can we leave these girls here in your safe keeping?'

'Sure, Marshal. Me and the wife'll look out for 'em.'

'Good, thanks.' Kirkpatrick turned to Thora. 'We'll be as quick as we can. Keep in your rooms. Don't go out.'

'We won't,' Thora said. She smiled, her spirits having picked up with the thought of a bath and clean clothes. 'You and Mr Pitt do what you have to. Come on, Lizzie, let's see what our room is like.' She took the girl's hand and, knowing Lizzie was still frightened, added, 'Won't it be nice to sleep in a proper bed? And not have to ride a horse for a while.'

She thought she would forever have nightmares about riding a horse, perched on the edge of the saddle, held there only by the arms of a smelly outlaw!

Kirkpatrick and Pitt walked back down to the general store, which had the grand name of Temple's Emporium. While quite small it was jam-packed with goods of all kinds so it was difficult to find a way through everything to the counter, behind which Temple and his wife stood ready to serve, and gossip with, their customers.

After Kirkpatrick quickly explained the situation, Mrs Temple hurried to sort out clothes for the two girls. Pitt helped her while her husband asked the marshal for more information.

'What were the names of the men who helped Hennessey?' he asked.

'It was two brothers called Frank and Jack O'Connor. Do you know them?'

Temple stroked his chin. 'Ain't sure. Be honest, Marshal, we get so many people through here, either miners looking for work or those wanting to make money off the miners, it's hard to remember all their names or faces. But if they used dynamite to get Hennessey out of jail then they must've been familiar with it, it ain't something most people would feel comfortable handling, and so ain't it likely that they've been miners at some point in their lives?'

'That's what we thought,' Kirkpatrick agreed.

'And if they were out to rob the Cotton Creek mine that also says to me they must have some idea of the lay-out of the place.' Temple thought for a moment then went on, 'But, Marshal, perhaps you're wrong because nothing ain't happened yet or Mr Fletcher, he's the mine manager, would've sent one of his men in to let me know. And it'd take a foolish man to rob the mine because of the guards employed there.'

'Well, I think Hennessey is so sure of himself that he's foolhardy,' Kirkpatrick said. 'And I don't know anything about the other two though they must be foolish if they're helping Hennessey. We'd better ride out to the mine. Warn this Fletcher.'

'Wish I could send someone with you.'

'It's OK. How do we get there?'

'Just follow the road on out of town and then keep on it. It won't take you long. It's only a couple of miles. You can't miss it. Hell, I sure do hope everything is OK.'

'We'll soon find out,' Pitt said, coming back to the counter to pay for his purchases. 'Mrs Temple, will you take everything over to Miss Dowling at the hotel and explain to her where we've gone?'

'Sure, honey.'

★ ★ ★

Thora had spent a long time relaxing in the tin-bathful of lovely hot water, washing her hair and scrubbing her body again and again until not even a speck of dirt remained.

Now she stood in the bedroom in front of the narrow piece of glass that served as a mirror looking at the skirt and jacket supplied by Mrs Temple. They weren't in the least bit fashionable and were too big. Lizzie looked much nicer in her dress and shawl. And although she knew she was being silly Thora couldn't help but be annoyed that Mr Pitt, and Ralph, thought she should wear a tailored costume in dull grey while they had purchased a pretty blue dress for Lizzie.

She immediately felt ashamed of herself. She was clean and smelt fresh and was wearing new clothes. She was no longer a prisoner of Old Man Hennessey. What else did she want?

Ralph by her side for one thing; how could she think of herself when he might still be in danger?

Oh, how she wished this was over, that Ralph and Mr Pitt hadn't gone chasing after Hennessey and the O'Connors.

But she was determined not to say anything, nor to show her fears, to anyone; not even Lizzie. Ralph had a job to do and it was up to her to support him.

22

After a while Hennessey and the O'Connors came to a halt by some low rocks so they could count the money. Pleased with themselves, Frank and Jack could hardly wait to find out how much they'd stolen and they quickly pulled the bills out of the saddle-bags. Hennessey elbowed them out of the way and took charge of the counting. When he'd finished he turned a furious face on the brothers.

'Two thousand dollars! That's all! Two thousand measly dollars. I don't believe it.'

'We done said it might be no more than that,' Jack protested.

Hennessey turned on him so fast he almost knocked him over. 'You also damn well said that they usually carried more money to buy special equipment. Something like that you told me. You said it could be as much as five thousand dollars. Led me to believe it would be worthwhile me riding into Arizona and endangering my life to do this job, while I wanted to go down into Mexico where I'd be amongst friends and I could plot my revenge on Felicidad. I agreed to do what you wanted and for what? I might've known better. You're nothing but fools.'

Neither Frank nor Jack could understand why Hennessey was making such a fuss. To them $2000 was a fortune, well worth the risk they'd run in stealing it. It was much more than they'd ever stolen before. With all that money they could do anything, go anywhere. And they'd got away with it. Old Man Hennessey evidently felt completely different.

'Two thousand dollars!' In a filthy temper he threw the money he held to the ground.

'Hey! Don't do that,' Frank cried, and quickly he and Jack began to scrabble around to collect it up before it was blown away. 'Hell, Bernie, you can damn well go into Mexico now with your share of . . . ' He came to a halt to work out a third of $2000.

'I used to earn double this on a rustling trip to Mexico. And I didn't have to share it with no one but my kids.'

'Seven hundred dollars,' Jack provided the answer.

Hennessey's eyes shone furiously. 'What the hell d'you mean? Seven hundred dollars! That ain't half.'

'Why should you have half?' Frank said. 'We never mentioned a half! It's to be shared between the three of us. I thought you'd know that. We all took the same chances. You're getting a third.'

'You two idiots don't deserve two-thirds. I done all the work.'

'How the hell do you make that out?' Jack was getting as angry as Hennessey. 'It was our plan. You didn't know nothing 'bout it till we done told you.'

'Wish you never had.'

'And if it wasn't for us you'd still be in jail,' Frank added, clenching his hands at his sides. 'In fact you'd've been hanged by now and buried in the ground.'

'OK, OK,' Hennessey said, pretending to calm down. 'OK. We'll share it three ways, like you say. I guess seven hundred dollars is better'n nothing.'

* * *

The Cotton Creek Copper & Silver Mining Company was a substantial place. There was a bunkhouse and several huts for the mine workers as well as a cookhouse and a tiny saloon situated in a tent, while the office was in a larger hut off to one side. The yard was littered with mining equipment, some of it reasonably new, some no more than broken pieces rusting from disuse. The entrance to the mine itself was out of sight on the far side of an incline. A number of miners stood about the place talking or making their way from the cookhouse where they had obviously just finished their midday meal. It made Pitt hope that before they did much else he and Kirkpatrick too could have something to eat and drink.

Other heavily armed men with sharp eyes patrolled the area, some on foot, some on horseback.

Pitt looked at Kirkpatrick and raised his eyebrows. 'Don't look like there's been a robbery.'

'Perhaps Thora was wrong. Or perhaps for some reason Hennessey and the O'Connors haven't gotten around to committing the robbery yet. Although,' Kirkpatrick added with a frown, 'I can't think of any reason why they should delay.'

'They could be watching the place,' Pitt said. 'And with so many guards about they might decide not to go ahead. Look, Ralph, there's a telegraph line going into the office. Would Mr Toombs maybe have sent a message here and so warned them to be on the lookout for Hennessey and his pals?'

'I doubt it. He'd only send messages to those towns that have lawmen. Come on, let's go and talk to the manager.'

Watched by a burly guard who made it plain he was quite willing to shoot first and ask any questions later, they dismounted in front of the office and, leaving their horses tied to the hitching rail, went inside. The room was square and filled with several chairs, two desks, both of which were overflowing with papers, and cupboards against the walls. It was also cool after the heat of the day outside.

Adam Fletcher, the mine manager, was in his early fifties, a short and tubby man with a harassed expression. He looked up at their entrance and got to his feet.

Quickly Kirkpatrick introduced himself and Pitt, at which Fletcher looked puzzled as well as anxious. He didn't like visits from lawmen; they meant trouble.

'How can I help you?'

'We're chasing three men, one of

whom is Bernie Hennessey . . . ' Kirk-patrick paused and Fletcher nodded to say he had heard of the man and his reputation; clearly he hadn't received a telegram from Mr Toombs. ' . . . We believe they're on their way to rob you.'

'Rob the mine?' Fletcher asked in a squeaky, surprised tone.

'Yes, sir. That's our understanding. They're certainly out to rob a silver mine somewhere and we think it's this one, especially as this was the direction in which they were headed. Quite honestly we're surprised the robbery hasn't taken place already.'

Fletcher laughed, a little nervously. 'As you can see for yourself, it hasn't. Things are quiet at the moment. That's not to say outlaws haven't robbed us in the past, which is why the mine's owners agreed to me employing several guards. Not many outlaws are willing to go up against such well-armed men. But . . . ' he came to a halt and frowned as if he had suddenly thought of something.

'What is it?' Pitt asked.

'Well, I . . . ' Fletcher turned pale. 'That is, Archie Wymark, my assistant manager, left a few days ago to pick up the mine payroll from Tucson.'

Kirkpatrick and Pitt looked at one another and Kirkpatrick said, 'He's overdue, is he?'

'Yes, he should've been back much earlier than this. But he's been late before because there are sometimes delays in Tucson or on the trail.' Fletcher frowned again. 'I admit I was starting to get worried.' He crossed over to the window and stared out, perhaps hoping Wymark would ride into the yard at that very moment.

'It's quite likely Hennessey was after the payroll not the silver,' Pitt said. 'Isn't it?' He looked at Kirkpatrick.

'It would certainly make an easier target,' Fletcher agreed. He ran a hand through his balding hair. 'Oh God, do you think that's what's happened?'

'I think we should find out,' Kirkpatrick decided. 'Although if that is the robbery they were planning it's happened by now.' All they could do was pick up the pieces.

'I'll come with you.' Fletcher got to his feet. 'With some men.'

As they went to the door, Kirkpatrick said, 'How many men did Wymark have with him?'

'Two miners and a guard. All of them are armed and reliable. Perhaps I should have sent more ... but it's always seemed more important to have the guards here ... there's never been trouble before ... ' Fletcher's voice trailed away.

Neither Kirkpatrick nor Pitt said anything about shutting the stable door after the horse had bolted, but both thought it.

'God, I hope nothing's happened to Wymark or the others. Or the money. The miners'll want paying.'

'We might be wrong,' Kirkpatrick said, but he didn't think so.

23

As well as Fletcher and three miners, a guard from the mine called Tom accompanied Pitt and Kirkpatrick.

Believing that the mine payroll was his responsibility Tom made sure he was out in front. Now he stopped at the top of a hill and turning in his saddle, called out, 'Here, Mr Fletcher, here they are.'

For a moment everyone else thought Tom meant that Wymark and the other three were riding towards them, alive and well, but that hope quickly faded as he continued, 'It looks like they're all dead.'

'Oh no.' Fletcher kicked his horse forward. He groaned. 'This is awful.'

Kirkpatrick and Pitt rode after him.

The far side of the hill was steep and almost bare, except for a scattering of boulders and clumps of sage-brush and grass. Lying unmoving on the slope were three bodies. There was no sign of any horses.

'Three men.' Fletcher called across to the guard, 'Tom, is Archie Wymark one of them?'

'I don't think so, sir. But there were definitely four men in the group. I watched 'em ride out.'

'Where is he? Perhaps he's all right. Oh God, I hope so.'

Pitt beckoned to them from where he was examining marks of horses and men by some rocks. 'I reckon this is where Hennessey and the O'Connors set up their ambush.'

'It'd be a good spot,' Kirkpatrick agreed.

'And now three men are dead. And the payroll has gone.' Fletcher spoke bitterly. He had tears in his eyes. 'How could it happen?'

'Hennessey is skilled at robbing people and it seems the other two are as well,' Kirkpatrick said.

'I wish you'd killed Hennessey when

you had the chance.'

'Mr Fletcher, not nearly as much as I do.'

As they rode down the hill, they stopped by the bodies only to confirm what they already knew: that each man was dead. It was when they were near to the bottom that Pitt came to a halt.

'What is it?'

'Over there, Ralph, amongst those rocks, someone's there.'

Everyone immediately drew their guns out from holsters, ready for trouble.

'No, wait.' Fletcher raised a hand. 'I recognize those clothes. It's Archie!'

He dismounted and followed by the others hurried over to the man.

'He's alive,' Fletcher cried out in relief. Wymark lay still and bleeding, breathing shallowly, but he was breathing. 'Archie, can you hear me?'

Wymark groaned and his eyelids flickered but he didn't regain consciousness.

Kirkpatrick bent over the man to

examine him. 'He's been shot in the leg. And it looks like his arm's broken.'

'He's lost a lot of blood,' Pitt added. 'Although the wound looks as if it's almost stopped bleeding now.'

'He must be all right,' Fletcher said, wiping Wymark's face with his bandanna.

Kirkpatrick straightened. 'Is there anyone in Cotton Creek who can look after him?'

'The Temples are skilled at doctoring. Well, as skilled as anyone around here. And I'm used to dealing with accidents at the mine.' Even as Fletcher spoke he took off his jacket and laid it across Wymark to keep him warm.

'Then I think you'd best take him back to town as quickly as possible.'

'I should come with you to look for Hennessey and the money.' Fletcher was torn between the two.

'There's no need. That's a job for the law. Hennessey is my responsibility and catching him my main concern. Your duty is to look after your man.'

'Mr Fletcher, I can go with them,' Tom added.

'All right.'

Kirkpatrick glanced at Pitt. 'What about you, Elias? I wouldn't blame you if you wanted to go back to Cotton Creek and Lizzie.'

'No, I'll see this through.'

'Thanks.' Kirkpatrick wasn't really pleased that the guard was going to accompany them. Although Tom was an extra gun to help them and, seeming a reliable sort, wouldn't slow them down, he didn't want any witnesses, besides Pitt, when he killed Old Man Hennessey.

'Will the three of you be enough?'

'Yes, don't worry about us. Will you explain to Miss Dowling at the hotel what I'm doing?'

'Of course.'

As Kirkpatrick, Pitt and Tom rode away, Fletcher ordered the remaining miners to help him with Wymark. They found a piece of cloth to tie a crude bandage around the wound in his leg to stop the bleeding and wrapped a saddle blanket around his shoulders. Then they hoisted him up on one of the horses and a miner quickly mounted up behind, holding him carefully in place.

'What about the others? Do we bury them here or should we take them back to the mine?'

For a moment Fletcher didn't look as if he knew what to do and the third miner said, 'None of 'em had family at the mine, or at Cotton Creek.'

Fletcher made up his mind. 'Then it might be best to bury them here, but first let's get Archie back to town. I don't like leaving these men out here dead like they are but nothing can hurt them now. Whereas if we don't get Archie help quickly he could die as well.'

'I could stop here with 'em,' the miner offered. 'Keep off any predators.'

'OK. Once we reach town I'll send some more men out from the mine to help you bury these poor bastards.' Fletcher would come back as well so that he could say a few words over them. It was the least he could do.

The tracks of Hennessey and the O'Connors were quickly found and followed.

'Looks like they decided to take along the extra horses,' Pitt said. 'Probably to sell.'

'I wonder if they'll split up now, or whether the O'Connors will go along with Hennessey. Or perhaps I should say whether Hennessey will go along with them.' Kirkpatrick paused. 'I can't see any reason why they should stay together.'

They had been riding for almost an hour when they heard the faint sound of shots from somewhere up ahead. They came to a halt and looked at one another.

'Hennessey?' Pitt asked.

'Who else?' Kirkpatrick took hold of his rifle. 'Let's go deal with the bastard once and for all.'

As Hennessey and the O'Connors were getting ready to ride again after resting up during the worst of the heat, Frank decided that the time and place were both right to split up with Bernie, let him go his way and he and Jack theirs.

'Bernie, we ain't coming to Mexico with you. There ain't no reason to. We're goin' back to Texas. So we'll go our separate ways iffen you don't mind.'

'No, I don't mind at all,' Hennessey growled, a threatening note in his voice.

'Hey!' Jack cried out. 'Nooo!'

His heart beating hard — what was wrong? — Frank swung round. Saw that Jack, a panicked look on his face, was clawing at his holstered gun. And that Hennessey, rifle pointing in his brother's direction, was about to betray them both. Jack never made it. Hennessey fired and, with a cry of pain that was abruptly cut off, Jack collapsed back on to the ground.

Frank reached for his own gun but he never made it either. Hennessey turned towards him, firing several times as he

211

did so. Frank's body was picked up, tossed through the air and slammed back down. His legs kicked once, twice, and then he was still.

'Serve you both damn right,' Hennessey said, a pleased expression on his face. 'Should never've tried to fool me. I ain't a fool and never have been.'

He went over to the horses and crammed all the money, all $2000 of it, so much better than $700 he thought with a grin, into one saddle-bag, which he took over to his horse. He wondered what to do with the spare animals. It would mean more money if he took them along to sell in Mexico but at the same time they would slow him down. In the end he decided to take just one with him in case anything happened to the animal he was riding. The rest he'd leave behind.

Grinning, he mounted his horse and, as he passed the bodies of the two O'Connor brothers, he said, 'And you idiots shoulda known by now that I never had any intention of sharing

anything with you. I am Old Man
Hennessey after all.'

And everything had, as usual, worked
out for him.

Laughing aloud he rode away.

24

'Miss Dowling.' Lizzie came into the bedroom she and Thora were sharing. 'Riders are coming.'

'Ralph?'

Thora's heart lightened then sank as Lizzie said, 'I don't think so. I couldn't see him or Elias. Shall we go find out?'

Arm in arm they went down the stairs and out of the door where the hotel clerk joined them.

'The man in the lead is Mr Fletcher, the mine manager. Lordy, looks like someone's been hurt.'

Thora clutched Lizzie's hand as she prayed it wasn't Ralph.

The clerk leant forward, peering down the road, shading his eyes against the afternoon sun. As the riders came closer he went on, 'Oh no, it's Archie Wymark.' He turned to the girls. 'He's the assistant manager and is in charge of collecting the mine payroll.'

'I bet that's what Hennessey and the others were going after,' Thora said, sorry for the injured man but relieved it was neither Ralph nor Mr Pitt.

'Seems they were successful,' the clerk muttered darkly, perhaps thinking that if so most of the miners wouldn't be able to pay the bills they had run up in town.

As the group of men neared the hotel, Fletcher turned his horse towards them. 'Are you Miss Dowling and her friend, Lizzie?'

'That's right.'

'Marshal Kirkpatrick and Mr Pitt, along with one of my guards, have gone after Hennessey. He asked me to tell you.'

Thora shut her eyes for a moment. Was this nightmare never going to end?

'Is Wymark hurt bad?' the clerk said.

'Bad enough.'

'Is there anything we can do?' Lizzie asked.

'I'm not sure. We're taking him to Mr

Temple. He might need help.'

'Miss Dowling, shall we find out?'

Thora nodded. Anything to keep busy. Anything to stop thinking. They followed the riders down the street to the store where Temple, alerted that he was needed, waited for them. He looked very concerned.

Wymark, who was still unconscious, was carried through to a room at the back where he was laid on a bed. Asking to be kept informed of his condition, Fletcher and the miners went off to the saloon for a drink, prior to returning to the mine to sort out everything there.

'Will he be all right?'

'I hope so, Miss Dowling. God! He's a good friend of mine.' Temple ran a hand through his hair and took hold of himself. 'Lizzie, can you help me undress him? And, Miss Dowling, perhaps you'll ask my wife to boil up some water and give you several clean towels as well as an old sheet to lay on the bed to soak up the blood.'

Oh dear, Thora thought heading for the door. Blood! Would she manage without being sick?

'I'll also need something to use as splints for his arm.'

Thora found that Mrs Temple, used to dealing with emergencies, was already heating up water and getting out towels and a sheet.

It wasn't long before she wished she hadn't been willing to agree to help Lizzie and Mr Temple. She supposed that as the wife of a lawman she might at some time need to doctor people who were hurt, but if her reaction to this situation was anything to go by she hoped that would never happen.

Although she'd never considered herself squeamish, as Temple probed for the bullet still in the man's leg, and as Wymark groaned and thrashed about, she had to swallow hard and avert her eyes. She hoped she wouldn't show herself up by being sick or fainting or making Mr Temple waste his time caring for her instead of Wymark.

Lizzie didn't seem particularly worried, following the man's orders without flinching, so Thora tried her best to conceal her discomfort.

It seemed an awfully long time before Temple exclaimed, 'Got it!' And he dropped the heavy slug in the bowl of bloody water.

Thora breathed a sigh of relief and made herself unclench her hands and stop gritting her teeth.

'Now all we have to do is wash the wound and bind it up to keep it clean and make sure it doesn't bleed any more. Then set his broken arm.' Temple made it sound very easy. 'Where are those bandages, Miss Dowling?'

'Here.' She handed across some strips torn from a clean sheet.

Lizzie pushed back a lock of Wymark's hair that had fallen into his eyes. 'Will he recover?'

Temple frowned. 'He's reasonably young and strong. And the wound wasn't particularly deep although he had lost some blood. Luckily he wasn't left out in the open long. I wouldn't have given much for his chances if he'd been out all night in the cold. As for the break in his arm' — the man shrugged — 'I don't think he'll lose it. We can only hope and pray.' He sounded matter-of-fact but there was deep anxiety in his eyes.

'Can he stay with you?' Lizzie said.

'Yeah, of course. We keep spare pillows and blankets here for this kind of thing and that way me and the wife can keep an eye on him. Let's take the old sheet away and make him comfortable.'

'Is there anyone who should be told?' Thora asked. 'I mean, has he a wife or family?'

Temple shook his head. 'No, Archie is a widower and has no children.'

Lizzie spoke shyly. 'Would it be OK if I was to sit with him?'

'Why, of course, it would.' Temple sounded a little surprised but pleased as well. 'That'd certainly help us. That way we won't have to keep looking in on him and he won't be left alone.'

'Will you mind, Miss Dowling?'

'No, Lizzie, that's all right.' Thora was surprised as well. She hadn't considered that Lizzie would be capable of nursing someone or would want to do so. 'I'll go back to the hotel. What about your dinner?'

'My wife'll provide that, don't worry. There, that's everything done. Come along, Archie, don't you dare die on me.' Temple put a pillow under the man's head and pulled a blanket over him. 'I need you.'

'Lizzie, I'll see you in the morning,' Thora said, going to the door with Temple. 'I'll be thinking of you and praying for Mr Wymark.'

And for Ralph and Mr Pitt.

'Miss Dowling,' Lizzie called her back.

'Yes?'

Lizzie made sure the door had shut behind Temple before she said, 'You won't tell anyone here about me, will you? What I am, or I mean what I was and do not want to be again. No one needs to know about my past, do they?'

'Of course they don't! I won't say a word. I promise. And nor will Ralph or Mr Pitt.'

'People won't guess though, will they? What about the bruises on my face? Won't they wonder how I got 'em?'

'I'm sure everyone will think they're just a result of Hennessey kidnapping the pair of us. I've got plenty of bruises on my arms. We both had torn clothes.' Thora looked at the girl in her pretty dress and the way her hair flowed down around her shoulders. 'No one would ever guess what you were in Felicidad.'

'Thank you,' Lizzie said with a little smile.

Alone with her patient she settled back in the chair prepared to start her long vigil.

And Thora said goodbye to Mr and Mrs Temple and walked back to the hotel, prepared to spend her time alone and lonely, thinking of Ralph.

25

'Sir, horses up ahead,' Tom said. 'I count five of 'em.'

'Me too.' Kirkpatrick nodded. 'That means there's two missing.'

They rode forward more cautiously now, eyes raking the landscape in all directions.

'Ralph,' Pitt said, 'looks like there are a couple of dead men.' He and Kirkpatrick glanced at one another.

The miners' horses took little notice of the arrival of the three men when they rode up and dismounted.

'Is one of 'em this Hennessey?' Tom asked, looking at the two bodies.

'No, more's the pity,' Kirkpatrick said. 'They must be the two O'Connor brothers. So much for helping Hennessey escape. He's turned on them like I thought he might. Be alert. The bastard's probably still around.'

'This one is still alive,' Pitt called from where he was bent over Jack O'Connor. He hunkered down by the man who opened his eyes. 'But not for much longer,' he added.

'Water,' Jack croaked.

Kirkpatrick handed Pitt his canteen and Pitt let Jack sip some of the water.

The outlaw flopped back. 'Thanks, mister.'

'What happened here?' Pitt asked.

'Hennessey, the bastard, shot us and took the money. Mister, is my brother dead?'

Kirkpatrick nodded and coming closer said, 'Yes, he is. I'm sorry. He didn't suffer.'

Jack seemed to find a little comfort in that. 'You all after Hennessey?'

'Yeah. Have you any idea where he's gone?'

'Mexico. He kept talking 'bout Mexico. And wanting revenge on Felicidad. Mister.' Jack's eyes sought Kirkpatrick's. 'We never meant no harm to them girls. Frank and me never touched 'em.' And with a little sigh the man died.

Kirkpatrick gave a sigh of his own. 'I'd almost feel sorry for him and his brother being betrayed like they have, were it not for the fact that they were willing to rob and kill.'

And even if they hadn't hurt Thora and Lizzie, they hadn't helped them either.

'They don't deserve any sympathy,' Pitt said bluntly. 'What shall we do?' He glanced up at the sky where buzzards scenting dead prey were already gathering, circling round.

Despite that, he didn't want to waste time burying these two before heading out after Hennessey and he was relieved when Kirkpatrick said, 'We should ride in search of the Old Man before he gets too far ahead.' The marshal looked along the way Hennessey must have taken. Perhaps now, surely, he couldn't be too far ahead. 'Tom, can you ride back to Cotton Creek? Tell Fletcher the latest news. And take these horses back to the mine. There's only Hennessey to face now; Elias and me can manage on our own.'

Tom was reluctant, obviously wanting to go after the murderer of some of his friends and get the payroll back, but in the end he nodded. 'OK.'

'And send out messages over the telegraph to any local law officers about the robbery and the fact that Hennessey is probably on his way to the border. They'll already know about his break out of jail. You could also send one to Mr Toombs at Felicidad, letting him know where we are and what's happening. Tell him the girls are safe.'

Tom nodded again. 'Mr Fletcher will do all that. Good luck, Marshal, Mr Pitt.'

'Thanks.'

★　★　★

Hennessey rode along slowly, laughing to himself at the way things had worked out in his favour. He was on his way to

Mexico, at last, with $2000 in his pocket. Not a large sum admittedly, but enough to tide him over until he'd decided what to do, where to go. And he was free of those idiots, the O'Connor brothers. How dare they think they could use him for their stupid schemes and he wouldn't mind! Or even realize what they were up to. He was Old Man Hennessey, not some stupid greenhorn, wet behind his ears.

But he hadn't ridden very far when his good mood and good humour gave way to a growing bad temper.

It was hot and dusty. He had a long and uncomfortable ride in front of him. He didn't have any whiskey with him because Frank hadn't wanted to attract attention to their presence by going into the general store. Worse, he was alone, with no one to share and applaud his cleverness. His kids, Bobby-Jo and Belle, were dead. OK, so they hadn't been up to much and he couldn't say he missed them, but they had been Hennesseys. And they'd been killed by the cowards who skulked in Felicidad. And he hadn't done anything about it because he was on the run, like a dog with its tail between its legs.

With a snarl he pulled his horse to a halt. Felicidad wanted seeing to and by God he was going to make the place pay.

Which was when he saw the dust on his backtrail. Hell! Someone was following him, already! Leaving the spare horse out of sight he rode to the top of the hill and stared back. His mouth gaped open. Kirkpatrick and Pitt! How the hell . . . it wasn't possible . . . yet there they were! He didn't waste long in wondering about their presence. They were alone; he could see a third man, who must have been with them, in the distance heading back towards Cotton Creek. Doubtless they believed they could handle a lone Hennessey. It would be a pleasure to prove them wrong.

The man grinned. He'd wait till night and then take them by surprise. They'd never expect him to be so nearby. He'd kill them. Easy!

★ ★ ★

As night fell and Cotton Creek settled into darkness and quiet, Lizzie continued to sit by Wymark's bed. He lay asleep and breathing heavily. Mrs Temple had lit a candle for her and this stood on a table on the other side of the bed, along with a glass of water in case Wymark woke up and was thirsty.

A couple of times she stood up to stretch and look out of the window, although there was little to see; no one was about, no noise or light came from any of the buildings. Everything had shut down early whereas Felicidad's redlight district would still be full of men enjoying themselves, wanting her. She decided she didn't miss it, or them, not one little bit!

She had never before been in such a small town, nor one so quiet, nor a place where good folks like Mr and Mrs

Temple treated her with respect. That she knew was mostly because of Miss Dowling who treated her almost as an equal; had done so even before they'd gone through so much together.

Wymark groaned and Lizzie moved closer to him. His eyes flickered open and focused on her.

'Are you an angel?'

Lizzie giggled. Hardly, unless she was a fallen one!

'How are you feeling?' she asked.

'Everything seems to hurt.'

'Don't try to move.' Lizzie pushed him gently back down on the pillow. 'You were shot and you broke your arm. But now you're safe in Cotton Creek. In Mr Temple's general store. Would you like a drink?'

'Yeah, please.'

Lizzie picked up the glass of water. Supporting Wymark's head in one arm, she put the glass to his lips.

'Not too much,' she warned.

'Who are you?'

'My name's Lizzie.'

'I don't know you, do I?'

'No. Now, hush, go back to sleep.'

'You won't leave me will you?'

'No,' Lizzie agreed with a smile.

'Good,' said Wymark. 'I'd like you to be here when I wake up.' He closed his eyes.

'I promise I will be.'

★ ★ ★

'You seen any sign of Hennessey yet?' Pitt asked, as Kirkpatrick brought his horse to a halt.

'No, but he's around here somewhere. I can almost smell him.'

'Me too.'

'Even so this looks like a good place to stop for the night, don't you think?'

Pitt looked round. They were at the bottom of a hill where there were rocks and boulders and plenty of scrub for a fire. 'Sure do,' he said and got off his horse.

26

Hennessey grinned. Those two idiots, the Eastern greenhorn who thought he could be a Western marshal, and the fancy gambler, who made a living out of playing poker, had fallen right into his trap! They had ridden on into the night and now there they were camped out at the bottom of the hill, fast asleep, with a camp-fire lighting up the blackness. They'd made clear targets of themselves!

He took hold of the rifle and crept slowly down towards them, pausing now and then to make sure he hadn't alerted either man to his presence. But he reached the base of the hill without them so much as stirring. Fools!

He stepped up to the fire and raised his rifle. One shot into each body so they would be dead almost before they knew what was happening. He wished it could be otherwise, that he could prolong their deaths, make each man realize they were going to die and why and at whose hand, but this way they didn't stand a chance!

He aimed and fired first at one then at the other. Yelling, he proceeded to shoot until his rifle was empty. Only then did he come to a halt, panting with the effort.

And that was when he knew he'd made a mistake.

'Got no more cartridges, Bernie?' Kirkpatrick said, and stepped out from behind the rock where he'd been hiding.

Hennessey whirled round. From out of the corner of his eye he saw Pitt emerge from some boulders on the far side of the little camp. He was caught between the two. With a snarl he threw the rifle on to the ground and raised both hands in the air.

'You really didn't think we were stupid enough to be asleep out here, lit up by a fire, when we knew you were in the vicinity did you?' Kirkpatrick mocked. 'Oh, but you did, didn't you? Really, Old Man, tut tut.'

'I surrender.'

'Go to hell, Bernie,' Kirkpatrick said.

'You can't shoot me,' Hennessey cried out in panic. 'I'm surrendering to you.'

For a moment Kirkpatrick, the lawman, hesitated.

'Don't listen to the bastard.' Pitt fired his gun.

And even as he did so, Kirkpatrick, the man, took over. He fired almost at the same time.

Hennessey's body was jerked this way and that. He fell with a thump on to the camp-fire and the smell of smouldering flesh filled the air.

Kirkpatrick went up to him and kicked his body off the fire. To his amazement there still remained a little life in the man's eyes.

Pitt said, 'This is for Lizzie and Miss Dowling,' and shot him in the forehead. Maybe in the weeks ahead he would come to regret killing an unarmed man but right there and then he felt absolutely nothing except relief that it was over.

Kirkpatrick felt much the same. He said, 'In the morning we bury this bastard and those other two and then we head back to Cotton Creek, collect the girls and go home.'

Pitt nodded. He wanted to go back to gambling at The Silver Dollar and make enough money to move on to Santa Fe, where he might meet people who hadn't heard of Old Man Hennessey.

★ ★ ★

Thora knocked on the door and went inside the bedroom to find Archie Wymark sitting up in bed, resting against the pillows, and Lizzie bending towards him, smiling at something he'd said. Thora smiled as well, thinking that many a man might not mind the fact that Lizzie couldn't cook or sew if he was rewarded with one of her smiles.

After all, cooking and sewing could always be taught whereas a smile came naturally.

'Good afternoon, Mr Wymark, how are you feeling?'

'Better, thanks, Miss Dowling. Although my leg hurts and I won't be able to use my arm for a while.'

'I expect you'll find someone to help you.' Thora glanced at Lizzie who blushed.

'Lizzie has been busy telling me all that's been going on.' Wymark shook his head. 'I saw three good men get shot. They didn't stand a chance. And the payroll has gone. It's hard to believe that Hennessey targetted the mine.'

'I think that was the O'Connor brothers' idea,' Thora said. 'And because of it people were killed in Felicidad as well, including my fiancé's deputy. Hennessey boasted about it all.'

'He has much to answer for, not least abducting you and Lizzie.' Wymark's hand slid across the bedclothes and Lizzie took hold of it.

235

'Luckily he didn't have the chance to do us any harm, did he, Miss Dowling?' Lizzie's eyes sought Thora's and pleaded with her to lie.

'No, thankfully, he didn't. And he only took Lizzie because she happened to be with me at the time. I was the one he was after.'

'Well, you're both safe now.'

'Yes, thank God.'

'Miss Dowling.' Lizzie accompanied Thora out of the room.

'What is it?'

'I don't want to go back to Felicidad. You see, no one knows me here. They don't know what I was. I can start anew. Become someone else. And Cotton Creek looks a nice place. Somewhere I can forget the past. Whereas in Felicidad I'll have to go back to my old life and everyone will remember I was Bernie's property. And, Archie, Mr Wymark, is a good man. I feel safe with him.' Lizzie's eyes lit up. 'He's going to give up working at the mine and ask Mr Temple for a job in the store.'

'Oh, Lizzie.' Thora took the girl in her arms and hugged her. She felt a word of warning might be necessary. 'Are you sure it's what you want and that you won't be bored? This is such a small place where nothing much can ever happen and you'll be the wife of a storekeeper.'

'Miss Dowling, after all I've put up with in my life I can handle any amount of boredom coming my way.'

Thora smiled. 'Then in that case, dear, I'm pleased for you. You deserve some happiness.'

'Miss Dowling, I want to thank you for all you've done for me.'

'I haven't done anything.'

'You let me think that perhaps I could make something of myself. And you haven't given my past away. I'll never forget you.'

Tears came into Thora's eyes and for a moment the two girls clung together.

'Good luck, Lizzie.'

'You too, Miss Dowling.'

'Miss Dowling, Miss Dowling!' It was

Mrs Temple calling out for her. 'Oh, there you are.'

'What is it?' Thora's heart missed a beat but then she realized the woman was beaming.

'Marshal Kirkpatrick and Mr Pitt are riding down the road.'

Thora's eyes gleamed. 'Is anyone else with them? I mean what about Old Man Hennessey?'

'No, they're alone.'

'Lizzie?' Thora said, seeing the girl hanging back. 'What's the matter? Aren't you coming?'

'I don't want to see Elias again. Will you explain? Give him my love, I do love him sort of, but he's part of my old life. Archie is my life now.'

'I'll tell him, don't worry,' Thora said. 'You go back to Mr Wymark.' She waited until Lizzie had gone, thinking that she would probably never see her again then, her heart lifting, she hurried outside. 'Ralph!' she called and waved.

'Thora,' Kirkpatrick said as he rode up beside her, 'we're going home.'

Pitt didn't quite know how to feel when Thora told him about Lizzie's decision to stay in Cotton Creek and marry Archie Wymark. Of course he was pleased for her. After being involved with the likes of Hennessey and Jake Carney she deserved a quiet life with a quiet man who would treat her right. At the same time he couldn't help but feel sad, feel that he had let an opportunity for his own happiness pass by.

But that wasn't Lizzie's fault, it was his, and he would have to live with it. Being a poker player he was used to keeping a straight face and not revealing his feelings. So he said nothing to Kirkpatrick or Thora.

But even he felt his heart lifting as, at last, the streets of Felicidad came into view. He knew how excited and carefree the townspeople would be now they were free of the threat of Old Man Hennessey. The place would be different.

'Everyone will be pleased to see us,' he said.

'They certainly will,' Kirkpatrick agreed. Smiling across at Thora he kicked his horse forward.

THE END

We do hope that you have enjoyed reading this large print book.

Did you know that all of our titles are available for purchase?

We publish a wide range of high quality large print books including:
Romances, Mysteries, Classics
General Fiction
Non Fiction and Westerns

Special interest titles available in large print are:
The Little Oxford Dictionary
Music Book, Song Book
Hymn Book, Service Book

Also available from us courtesy of Oxford University Press:
Young Readers' Dictionary
(large print edition)
Young Readers' Thesaurus
(large print edition)

For further information or a free brochure, please contact us at:
Ulverscroft Large Print Books Ltd.,
The Green, Bradgate Road, Anstey,
Leicester, LE7 7FU, England.
Tel: (00 44) **0116 236 4325**
Fax: (00 44) **0116 234 0205**

SILVER GALORE

John Dyson

The mysterious southern belle, Careen Langridge, has come West to escape death threats from fanatical Confederates. Is she still being pursued? Should she marry Captain Robbie Randall? The Mexican Artiside Luna has his own plans . . . With gambler and fast-gun Luke Short he murders Randall's men and targets Careen. Can the amiable cowboy Tex Anderson and his pal, Pancho, impose rough justice as with guns blazing they go to Careen's aid?